Fuh Araki
ORIGINAL STORY Kennoji
CHARACTER DESIGN KWKM
6
SKILL
EGENDARY ASSASSIN

CONTENTS

The Guild Member with a Worthless Skill
Is Actually a Legendary Assassin

mission.
28
CLEANUP

SO YOU MEAN TO SAY HE WAS THE CULPRIT BEHIND THE INCIDENTS?
I SEE NOW.
IF ONLY WE'D HAD A HEALER AROUND...
OH, NO! IT'S ONLY NATURAL THAT HE ENDED UP—
...THEN I COULD HAVE FIXED HIM UP AND BROKEN HIM ALL OVER AGAIN.

THANK YOU FOR HEARING OUT MY REQUEST AND DOING THIS.
YOU IDENTIFIED THE CULPRIT AND EVEN DEALT WITH HIM...
I CANNOT TELL YOU HOW GRATEFUL I AM THAT MY PEOPLE ARE SAFE.
THE GUILD COULDN'T CONTINUE LOSING ITS ADVENTURERS EITHER.
ACCORDING TO WHAT I'VE HEARD, SEEING HOW THE PRISONERS OF WAR WERE TREATED...
...MIGHT HAVE PROMPTED HIS TENDENCIES.
I'LL LEAVE IT TO YOU TO INFORM THE DALTON FAMILY. THE SITUATION SHOULD BE CLEAR TO ANYONE WHO SEES THE SCENE.
IF YOU ENCOUNTER ANY ISSUES, I CAN ALSO HAVE A WORD WITH HIS MAJESTY.
THANK YOU SO VERY MUCH! YOU'VE DONE SO MUCH FOR ME, ROLAND-SAMA!
PLEASE LET ME REPAY YOU!
THAT'S ALL RIGHT.
IF YOU'LL EXCUSE US.

JARA (JINGLE) じゃ
YOU MIGHT AS WELL ACCEPT THINGS YOU'RE GIVEN.
I DIDN'T DO THIS FOR A REWARD.
...
HE WAS SCUM, BUT I MIGHT SYMPATHIZE WITH HIM A BIT.

IT WASN'T TOO UNCOMMON TO TORTURE PRISONERS DURING THE WAR, YOU KNOW.
YES, PEOPLE'S VALUES CHANGE AFTER WAR.
BUT I STILL HAVE ONE QUES-TION.
OH? WHAT'S THAT?
HOW DID SOMEONE LIKE HIM HYPNOTIZE YOU?
OH. HA HA...
VAMPIRES ARE AN EXTREME RACE. VERY MUCH SO.

A HUMAN'S ABILITIES WOULDN'T CHANGE MUCH AFTER STAYING UP THROUGH THE NIGHT, YES?
YOU DON'T MEAN...
HA-HA-HA. IT'S EXACTLY WHAT YOU THINK.
WHILE THE SUN SHINES, I'M VERY WEAK.
ESPE-CIALLY AGAINST MAGIC.
COME TO THINK OF IT, THE VAMPIRES ONLY FOUGHT AT NIGHT DURING THE WAR...
...SO THAT'S WHY I ASSOCIATE THEM WITH DARKNESS.
SO IN OTHER WORDS, FIRE GUARD JUST ALLOWS YOU TO FUNCTION IN LIGHT.
IN TERMS OF DEMONKIN RANKS...
...OUR POWER DROPS TO THAT OF A PLATOON LEADER.
TAKING ANY ACTION DURING THE DAY IS RISKY.
I SEE. NOW I UNDER-STAND.

SO ACTUALLY...
...I'VE NEVER TOLD A HUMAN ANY OF THIS BEFORE.
RIGHT, I WON'T GO AROUND TELLING OTHERS.
ALSO, I HAD...
...THIS TEENSY THOUGHT.
THAT MAN MIGHT NOT...
...HAVE EVEN KNOWN I WAS A VAMPIRE.
SHIRE (BLUNT)
...
ON THAT DAY, WHEN I WAS HEADED HOME AFTER FINISHING A QUEST...
...THE SUN WAS ALREADY COMING UP...
MOJI (FIDGET)
MOJI

THAT ONLY HAPPENED BECAUSE YOU ASSUMED HUMANS ARE INFERIOR LIFE-FORMS.
I REGRET THAT I DID...
OUCH!
TASHI (THUNK)
SO HE WAS JUST TRYING TO TAKE ADVANTAGE OF A PRETTY WOMAN THEN...
I GAVE THAT SADIST TOO MUCH CREDIT.
I VALUE YOUR ABILITIES AND HOW UNIQUE YOU ARE...
...SO DON'T WORRY ME TOO MUCH.
OH, WHAT A COMPLI-MENT...IT MAKES ME WANT TO BELIEVE YOU.
ASSUME ALL HUMANS YOU MEET ARE LIKE ME.
IF YOU DO THAT, THIS WON'T HAPPEN AGAIN.
WELL, THEN I SUPPOSE I REALLY CAN'T LET MY GUARD DOWN...

AHHH.
MAYBE I'LL FALL IN LOVE WITH EVERYONE THEN!
D'AWWW!
WHAT-EVER WILL I DO?
...ANYWAY, JUST DON'T LET YOUR GUARD DOWN.
ROLAND-SAMA...
LET ME JUST SAY AGAIN... THAT I REALLY AM GRATEFUL YOU CAME TO MY RESCUE.
HE WOULD HAVE KEPT FORCING ME TO DRINK BLOOD I'D NEVER TOUCH, AND I WOULD HAVE ENDED UP HIS SCAPEGOAT.

LOOKS LIKE HE UPSET A PICKY EATER.
WELL, IN A WAY...
BUT HE DID IT TO KEEP THE HYPNOSIS FROM BREAKING...
HE MADE ME DRINK BLOOD FOR SUCH A LOUSY REASON.
IT'S AN ACT MORE SACRED THAN SHARING A BED...
...AND HE FORCED ME TO DO IT TO A LOWER RACE WHILE I WASN'T MYSELF...
AHH... I CAN'T EVEN TELL YOU HOW HORRIBLE THAT IS...
BUT YOU SAVED ME FROM THAT HELL, ROLAND-SAMA.
I HARDLY DID ANYTHING.

GYU (SQUEEZE)
ぎゅ…
I THINK I GENUINELY UNDERSTAND WHY RILEYLA-SAMA LOVES YOU.
AFTER ALL, I CAN'T HELP FEELING THAT WAY TOO...
PIKU (TWITCH)
かぷっ
KAPU (CHOMP)
ぷはっ
PUHA (PWAH)
...?
YOU DIDN'T BITE ME? I DON'T MIND IF YOU DRINK A LITTLE.
ふる
FURU (SHAKE)
ふる
FURU
THIS IS A SHOW OF COURTSHIP.
BECAUSE VAMPIRES ARE STE-REOTYPED TO BITE...
... STOP-PING JUST BEFORE SHOWS THAT WE CARE FOR THE PERSON.

I, CANDICE MINELAD, GENUINELY ADORE YOU, ROLAND-SAMA.
WOULD YOU DO ME THE HONOR OF PARTAKING OF MY BLOOD?
I DON'T MIND, BUT DOES IT HAVE ANY SIGNIFICANCE IF I DO?
I BELONG TO YOU...
THAT'S WHAT IT WOULD MEAN.
PUTSU (NIP)
KOKUN (NOD)

AHH...
ROLAND-SAMA, THANK YOU...
I'M SO HAPPY...
HAAH... I WOULD HAVE NO REGRETS EVEN IF I TURNED TO DUST RIGHT NOW.

GO (RUMBLE)
WHAT ARE...
GO
GO
GO
GO

GO
GO
GO
GO
...YOU TWO DOING RIGHT IN FRONT OF OUR HOME!?
OH MY, OH MY.
IT'S NOT PROPER TO SPY ON OTHERS, RILEYLA-SAMA.
GO
GO
GO

ME!?
SPY!?
YOU ARE IN FRONT OF THE HOUSE!
BRAZENLY SO!
A-A-A-AND KISSING!
APPARENTLY, THAT'S HOW THE CEREMONY WORKS.

THE CEREMONY IS EXACTLY WHAT I TAKE ISSUE WITH!!!
BASA
BASA (FLAP)
BASA
BATAN (SHUT)
SHE'S ASLEEP?
YES.
IT SEEMS SHE WAS QUITE EXHAUSTED. SHE FELL INTO A SLUMBER UPON MEETING HER BED.

RILA, ACTUALLY, I...
'TIS FINE.
I COULD SENSE SOME-THING HAP-PENED.
YOU BOTH CAME BACK AT THIS HOUR...
...AND REEKED OF BLOOD AS WELL.
YOU WERE RIGHT ABOUT DEY.
YOU'RE A GOOD JUDGE OF PEOPLE.
YOU ONLY SAY THAT NOW?
GOSHI (CARESS)
YOU DON'T HAVE TO WAIT FOR ME TO COME HOME.
!
BUN (SHAKE)
BUN

I...UM...
...DID SO BECAUSE I SIMPLY WISHED TO.
EXCEPT I DIDN'T EXPECT THE SCENE I WITNESSED EARLIER.
PUUU (POUT)
BUT I AM GLAD THAT YOU...
...CAME HOME SAFELY, KNAVE.
SURE...

I'M GLAD TO BE BACK.

mission.
29
R&R TRIP, PART 1
ZAWA (CHATTER)
ザワ
ザワ
ZAWA
ザワ
ZAWA
SOWA (FIDGET)
そわ
SOWA
そわ
HISO (WHISPER)
HISO
ヒソヒソ
そわ
SOWA
SOWA
そわ

EVERYONE SEEMS ON EDGE.
IT'S BECAUSE PEOPLE ARE HERE FROM HEADQUARTERS. THREE OF THEM, ACTUALLY.
THAT'S QUITE A LOT.
DID SOMETHING HAPPEN?
POYAYAN (GLOOOW)
ぽややん
YEAH, MAYBE SOMETHING HAPPENED.
TCH.
STOP THAT AND GET BACK TO WORK.

MILIA-SAN!
HUH?

PACHI (CRACKLE)
PARA (CRUMBLE)
PARA
PACHI
PARA
PACHI
SHUUUUU (FSHHH)
ARE YOU ALL RIGHT, MILIA-SAN?
YES!
DID SOME-THING JUST EXPLODE?

HEEEY! IF ANYONE'S INJURED, WE'LL HEAL YOU.
I KNEW THINGS WERE GETTING TOO INTENSE.
THEY WERE GETTING WAY TOO HEATED FOR AN ARGUMENT.
IT WAS OVER AN AFFAIR.
THIS ISN'T THE PLACE FOR A FIGHT.
YEAH, SERIOUSLY.
LOOKS LIKE IT WAS A LOVERS' QUARREL BETWEEN AN ADVENTURER COUPLE.
...
NO, I THINK THAT WAS A DECOY TO DECEIVE US.
THEY WOULD HAVE STOOD OUT TOO MUCH ALONE.
AND THE ARGUMENT HIDES THEIR TRUE AIM.
WHAT ADULT WOULD CAUSE THIS MUCH DESTRUCTION JUST BECAUSE OF A LITTLE INFIDELITY?
OH!
AND IN A PLACE AS PUBLIC AS THIS?
THEY DIDN'T NEED TO DO THIS! WHAT WAS THE POINT!?
THEN WHO WAS THE TARGET? THEY DIDN'T INJURE ANY STAFF OR ADVENTURERS.
IF THEY WERE TRYING TO JUST DAMAGE THE BUILDING, THEY COULD HAVE ATTACKED FROM OUTSIDE.
NO...

IN THAT CASE...
IT WAS A RANDOM ACT OF TERROR.
WHOA! THE WHOLE PLACE GOT BLOWN AWAY.
COULD YOU HEAL THIS?
OKAY!
MY FAVORITE BAG CAUGHT ON FIRE!
WANT TO BUY A NEW ONE? I'LL GO WITH YOU.
HAAH... THAT WAS A SHOCK.
I'LL GO WITH YOU TOO.
I WOULDN'T EVEN EXPECT THIS DURING A QUEST.

WE NEED TO CAPTURE THE CULPRIT BEFORE THEY ESCAPE!
WAIT, ROLAND-SAN!
GYU (SQUEEZE)
S-S-S-S-SORRY!
WE DID IT!
WASN'T EXACTLY A MYSTERY, GUYS.
SEE?
IT REALLY WAS JUST A COUPLE'S FIGHT. RIGHT?
WH-WHAT HAP-PENED HERE!?
OH! IT'S THE BRANCH MANAGER! WE CAN ALL CALM DOWN!
WELL, WE CAN'T CHANGE WHAT HAPPENED ...

IT LOOKS LIKE THE TWO OF THEM REGRET THEIR ACTIONS.
WE'LL LET THEM OFF WITH A STERN WARNING THIS TIME.
NOW, AS FOR THE GUILD...
THE ADVENTURERS GUILD IS TEMPORARILY CLOSED FOR REPAIRS.
THOUGHT SO...
BUT WHAT WILL WE DO IN THE MEAN-TIME?
IT'S NOT LIKE ALL OF US CAN TAKE TIME OFF...
...
RIGHT.

THIS IS ODD TIMING...
BUT REMEMBER WE HAD VISITORS FROM HQ THIS MORNING?
THEY WANTED TO PRAISE OUR WORK AT THIS BRANCH.
AND THEY GAVE US A 500,000-RIN BONUS.
WHOA... WOW...
BUT WON'T THAT JUST GO TO REPAIRS?
OF COURSE NOT!
OH, THINKING ABOUT IT, I SUPPOSE THE TIMING WOULD HAVE LINED UP...
TIMING FOR WHAT?
I HAVE A PROPOSAL.

LET'S USE THIS MONEY FOR A COMPANY TRIP!
WOW! IT'S THE OCEAN, ROLAND-SAN! THE OCEAN!
HEY! THAT'S DANGER-OUS. GET BACK INSIDE!

I'M SORRY. IT'S JUST BEEN SO LONG SINCE I'VE LEFT LAHTI.
HEE-HEE.
REALLY NOW...
HMPH...
SHE'S SO EXCITED FOR SOMETHING AS PALTRY AS THE SEA.
BOSO
And who got so caught up at the beach, she lost her own coin purse?
BOSO (WHISPER)
NGH...
I'M SURPRISED YOU CAME, ROLAND.
YOU DON'T SEEM LIKE YOU'D BE UP FOR AN EVENT LIKE THIS.
...I PARTAKE FROM TIME TO TIME.
THEN I SHALL GO! YOU MAY STAY HOME AND WHILE AWAY YOUR TIME IN BOREDOM IF YOU WISH, KNAVE!
YOU REALIZE YOU CAN'T GO WITHOUT ME, RIGHT...?
SO...
WHAT A VERY FINE POSITION YOU'VE PUT YOURSELF IN—THE ONLY MAN IN A CARRIAGE FULL OF WOMEN.
BOSO
It was just a coincidence. Though as far as positions go...
...I do have my post as adventurer proctor—I'd say that's a fine position.
BOSO

IS IT REALLY?
WELL, I DID GET TO GO TO THE CAPITAL TO ATTEND A SEMINAR FOR IT.
I WENT TO THE CAPITAL FOR WORK AND SEMI-NARS...
JUST LIKE A NOR-MAL PERSON.
にやり
NIYARI (GRIN)
ALL THESE WORDS ABOUT MY PERFECTLY NORMAL JOB ARE JUST FLOWING OUT OF ME.
...
I THOUGHT I UNDERSTOOD HIS SENSE OF VALUES, BUT IT SEEMS I WAS MISTAKEN.
ROLAND-SAN, WHAT HAVE YOU BEEN MUTTERING ABOUT?
OH... NOTHING AT ALL.
GOSO (RUSTLE)
GOSO
DID YOU READ THE BROCHURE?
KOHTOKA, THE PLACE WE'RE GOING TO, IS A PORT TOWN.
I HEARD IT'S VERY BUSY AND HAS A LOT OF FISHING AND TRADE!

ARE YOU GOING TO SHOP, ROLAND-SAN?
NO, NOT REALLY.
YOU AREN'T?
OH! RIGHT, THERE'S ALSO A BEACH! I BROUGHT A SWIMSUIT. ♪
ACK! I FORGOT MINE!
IT'S FINE. LOOKS LIKE THERE ARE SHOPS.
DID YOU PREP IN ADVANCE, BRANCH MANAGER?
WHAT!?
N-N-N-NOT IN PARTIC-ULAR!
GUSHA (CRUMPLE)
OH! YOU'RE CHECKING OUT THE SHOPS!
SO YOU'RE GOING TO BUY ONE!
I-I-I'M NOT! I-I-I'M JUST CHECKING THE ROUTE! TO MAKE SURE WE'RE ON SCHEDULE!
...? SWIM... SUIT?
DO THEY NOT HAVE THEM IN HELL?

MAY I COME IN, ROLAND-SAN?
YES.

WOULD YOU LIKE TO LOOK AROUND TOWN?
WHY IS MISS PRIMA DONNA HERE!?
ONLY STAFF ARE SUPPOSED TO BE ON THIS TRIP!
DO NOT SWEAT THE DETAILS.
I KNOW! I SHALL GO PURCHASE ONE OF THOSE "SWIM SUITS" WITH MILIA!
HUH? BUT I WANTED ROLAND-SAN TO—
SORRY FOR IMPOSING. THANK YOU.
UGH. ALL RIGHT. IF I HAVE TO.
WE SHAN'T RETURN UNTIL WE FIND A SWIMSUIT BEFITTING MYSELF!
BATAN (SHUT)
IF SHE'S WITH MILIA, SHE SHOULDN'T GET LOST.

I'M COMING IN!
GACHARI (CHK)
ガチャリ…
MY OH MY, WHAT A SHOCK I HAD WHEN I SAW THE GUILD IN THAT STATE.
AND I HAD TO COME BACK TO THIS TOWN ALL OVER AGAIN.
I CAN'T BELIEVE A HUMAN LIKE YOU COULD WORK A VAMPIRE LIKE ME TO THE BONE, ROLAND-SAMA.
YOU ARE MINE, AREN'T YOU?
HA HA... I WAS JUST JOK-ING.
SO IS THIS ABOUT WHAT I ASKED YOU TO DO?
YES, THOUGH ASKING ME TO LOOK INTO AN INCREASE IN DRUG USERS WITHOUT ANYTHING ELSE TO GO ON...
...WAS A RATHER RIDICULOUS REQUEST.
POSU (POMF)
THE INTEL CAME FROM A FASTIDIOUS SOURCE. THAT REALLY MUST BE ALL SHE KNEW.
WELL, I'M LUCKY THE PLACE WAS AROUND KOHTOKA.
SINCE SO MANY PEOPLE ARE AROUND, I FOUND PLENTY OF INFO.

SURI (RUB)
SURI
A DRUG FITTING THE DESCRIPTION HAS BEEN MAKING THE ROUNDS IN THE PLEASURE DISTRICT.
MANY PEOPLE AND THINGS COME IN AND OUT OF KOHTOKA, SO IT MUST HAVE BEEN EASY TO BRING IN.
IT'S CALLED "SECOND," AND IT'S GOOD FOR A TEMPO-RARY HIGH, BUT IT'S TERRIBLY ADDICTIVE.
EVEN DISPELL DOESN'T REMOVE THE SIDE EFFECTS.
SOUNDS LIKE TROUBLE.
WHILE I WAS SCOPING THINGS OUT THESE PAST FEW DAYS, ONE STOREFRONT SEEMED SUSPICIOUS.
WILL YOU TAKE ME?
THE LETTER CAME FROM ELVIE.
ALL IT SAID WAS, "A NASTY DRUG HAS BEEN MAKING ITS WAY THROUGH THE COUNTRY. BE CAREFUL."
I CONSIDERED JUST WAITING TO SEE WHAT WOULD HAPPEN, BUT SOME PEOPLE WOULD INEVITABLY TRY IT OUT OF CURIOSITY.
I COULDN'T IGNORE THE POSSIBILITY IT WOULD EVENTUALLY GET TO MY TOWN.
R— REALLY?

I CAN MAKE A WHOLE 100,000 RIN IN JUST ONE DAY OF WORK!?
YES! THINK OF IT AS LIKE EARNING A LITTLE EASY SPENDING MONEY DURING YOUR VACATION!
HUH? OH MY?
ISN'T SHE FROM THE GUILD...?
DID THEY GET SEPARAT-ED?
WHAT AN INNOCENT COUNTRY GIRL.
APPARENTLY, SHE HASN'T LEFT HER HOMETOWN MUCH.
OH.
ROLAND-SAMA, THAT MAN TALKING TO HER...
SEVERAL PEOPLE SAID THEY GOT DRUGS FROM HIM.
I SEE... I CAN HANDLE THIS ALONE.
LOOK FOR RILA. SHE'S PROBABLY LOST SOME-WHERE.
OKAY!
BE CAREFUL OUT THERE!
WHO DO YOU THINK YOU'RE TALKING TO?

NOW, LET'S GET GOING. THE SHOP'S THIS WAY. I'LL TAKE YOU.
HUH?
GUI (TUG)
UH?
MISS... WAS IT MILIA-CHAN? ARE YOU EXPERIENCED?
IN WHAT?
OH! NOW I LIKE THAT REACTION! YOU MIGHT BE ABLE TO EARN EVEN MORE THEN!
HM?
FU (FWISH)
DAN (SLAM)
GAH!?
ROLAND-SAN!? WHAT ARE YOU DOING HERE?
MILIA-SAN, IF YOU GO WITH THIS MAN, HE'LL MAKE YOU DO UN-SPEAKABLE THINGS.
HUH!? WHO ARE YOU!?
WHAT!?

WHAT!? HE NEVER MENTIONED THAT!
OF COURSE NOT. IN THE WORST CASE, YOU MAY HAVE NEVER MADE IT HOME.
GI
GUGI (CRICK!)
GI
GI
WHAT...?
I NEED TO HAVE A CHAT WITH HIM, SO WHY DON'T YOU GO BACK TO THE INN?
THIS ISN'T A PLACE YOU SHOULD BE.
KA (THUNK)
WH- WHAT? BUT WHAT ABOUT YOU, ROLAND-SAN?
HURRY.
O- OKAY!
YOU! WHAT DO YOU THINK YOU'RE DOING!?
YOU THINK YOU'LL GET AWAY WITH THIS? HUH!?

STOP SHOUTING. I DON'T CARE WHO YOU ARE. I'D STILL DO THE SAME THING.
DO YOU KNOW ANYTHING ABOUT A DRUG NAMED SECOND?
HUH?
WHAT ARE YOU TALKING ABOUT?
PEKI (SNAP)
AGHHHH!?
I'LL ASK AGAIN.
FEIGN IGNORANCE, AND YOU'LL GET A SECOND TASTE OF THAT.
URGH... M-MY FINGER...
MY FINGER...
I TOLD YOU I DON'T KNOW.
I GUESS WE'LL SEE HOW MUCH YOU CAN HANDLE THEN.
W-W-W-WAIT! PLEASE WAIT!
ALL I'VE BEEN TOLD IS TO FIND GIRLS AND TO GIVE THEM THESE DRUGS THEY HANDED ME!
UGH...
URGH...
GACHI (CHATTER)
GACHI

WAIT! MAYBE IT'S THAT WHATEVER DRUG YOU'RE LOOKING FOR!
IT'S CALLED SECOND. ARE YOU THE ONLY ONE DIS-TRIBUTING IT?
NO, THERE ARE THREE OTHERS...
IT'S JUST AN APHRODISIAC. YOU DON'T HAVE TO BE SO INTENSE ABOUT IT...
YEEK! WHAT!?
THE STUFF YOU'RE DEALING ROTS PEOPLE FROM THE INSIDE OUT. IT'S AS GOOD AS POISON.
IF THEY KEEP TAKING IT, THEY DESTROY THEIR SENSE OF SELF AND FORGET WHO THEY EVEN ARE.
THE DRUG ROBS THEM OF THEIR *NORMAL* LIVES.
IF MORE PEOPLE FALL PREY TO IT, THEN SOON EVERYONE WILL BE DEPENDENT ON THE DRUG.
EVEN PEOPLE YOU KNOW, LIKE YOUR LOVED ONES AND FAMILY.
WHAT...? BUT THE MASTER SAID THE MONEY WOULD HELP THE TOWN...
IS THAT YOUR BOSS? WHERE IS HE?
HE...
HE'S A RED-HEADED MAN WITH SHARP EYES WHO COMES BY THE SHOP SOME-TIMES.
I DON'T KNOW WHO HE ACTUALLY IS OR WHERE HE CAME FROM.
JUST TELL ME WHAT YOU KNOW, AND TAKE ME TO THIS SHOP.

IT'S OVER HERE.
THE MASTER COMES BY TWICE A WEEK TO REPLENISH OUR STOCK.
I DUNNO WHERE IT'S BEING MADE OR WHERE HE'S BRINGING IN THE GOODS FROM.
BUT KOHTOKA HAS GOT TONS OF WAREHOUSES WITHOUT IDENTIFIABLE OWNERS.
HE MIGHT BE KEEPING IT IN ONE OF THOSE.
ACTUALLY, I HEARD SOMETHING ABOUT THE DRUGS FROM A GAL AT THE SHOP.
IT'S SUPPOSED TO FEEL AMAZING AFTER USING IT AND DOING THE DEED, SO THE CUSTOMERS AND GIRLS ARE BOTH HOOKED.
OH, RIGHT. I'LL TELL YOU THE GIRLS' PRICES.
IF ANYTHING HAPPENS, YOU CAN SAY A BARKER LED YOU OVER.
HERE'S THE SHOP.
OH, BUT THE MASTER WON'T BE HERE TODAY.
...
THIS IS GOOD ENOUGH.

IF YOU REALLY CARE ABOUT THE TOWN...
...THEN YOU'D BETTER GET RID OF THOSE DRUGS.
YES, SIR!!!
BISHI (SHWIP)
GOOD WORK!
HUH? MY FINGER ISN'T ACTUALLY BROKEN?
WAKI (WIGGLE) WAKI
A GATE.
IN COURT-RANK MAGIC, WHERE MONO IS HIGHEST, THIS IS PENTA RANK.
SINCE ROJE SAID SHE COULDN'T LEARN SHADOW, WHICH IS TETRA MAGIC...
...THIS DEMONKIN MUST BE AT HER LEVEL OR ABOVE.
WELL... I'LL JUST NEED TO SEE WHO IT IS THEN.

A HILL?
SO THE INN IS OVER THERE.
HEY!
WHO THE HELL ARE YOU!?
THIS IS BARON MARTY CUTHRA'S ABODE!
IF YOU HAVEN'T GOT BUSINESS HERE, THEN SCRAM!
A BARON… I SEE. SO THAT'S WHY THEY CLAIMED IT'D "BENEFIT" THE TOWN.
I DIDN'T EXPECT THE GOV-ERNING LORD TO HAVE A STAKE IN THIS.

SUTA (TMP)
SUTA
SUTA
H—
HEY! DON'T THINK YOU CAN JUST HIDE OVER THERE...
HUH?
WHERE DID HE GO?
FROM EXPERIENCE, MOST MANSION OWNERS CHOOSE A ROOM ON THE TOP FLOOR WITH A VIEW.
IN OTHER WORDS, THERE.

DAN (TMP)
WHAT THE—!?
GATA (KLAT)
SU (SHUMP)

WH-WHO ARE YOU!?
A GUEST.
D-DON'T SCREW WITH ME! WHAT KIND OF GUEST SUDDENLY APPEARS OUT OF NOWHERE ON THE THIRD FLOOR!?
S-SOMEONE, GET OVER HERE!
WHO DO YOU THINK STANDS TO BE IN A WORSE POSITION IF YOU CALL SOMEONE OVER?
WHAT? WHO THE HELL ARE YOU?
YOU DARE DO THIS KNOWING I'M MARTY CUTHRA!?
THAT'S RIGHT. I'M FROM THE KINGDOM OF FELIND'S SPECIAL PUBLIC WELFARE DIVISION.
SPECIAL... WHAT? I'VE NEVER HEARD OF THAT IN MY LIFE.
IT'S NOT A PUBLIC ORGANIZATION. WE'RE AN INTELLIGENCE UNIT THAT REPORTS DIRECTLY TO KING RANDOLF.
...FOR THIS SETUP.
Y-YOU REPORT DIRECTLY TO HIS MAJESTY!?
YES, IN THIS SETUP.
WHY ARE YOU GOING ON ABOUT SETUPS?
QUIET DOWN. YOU'RE MAKING THIS A CHORE.

I HEAR A SUSPICIOUS DRUG HAS BEEN SPREADING AROUND THIS REGION, SO I'VE LAUNCHED AN INVESTIGATION.
YOU MUST KNOW THAT RUBENS IS HAVING A SIMILAR PROBLEM.
I'LL NEED TO REPORT THIS TO HIS MAJESTY.
W-WAIT! YOU CAN'T CENSURE ME FOR...
...WHAT I DO IN MY OWN TERRITORY!
WHAT ARE YOU TALKING ABOUT? ALL LANDS, AND THEIR CIVILIANS, BELONG TO THE KINGDOM.
THE NOBILITY IS SIMPLY ALLOWED TO MANAGE IT IN THE KING'S PLACE.
ALLOWING SECOND TO RUN RAMPANT IS CRIMINAL. YOU WON'T BE LET OFF EASY.
URGH...
GU (CLENCH)
GU
GU
GU
GU
GU
HA!
WHAT ARE YOU TALKING ABOUT!?
THE PEASANTS ONLY EXIST TO MAKE THEIR LORD STINKING RICH!
THAT'S THE ONLY REASON WHY WE ALLOW THEM TO LIVE!

SHA (SWOOSH)
I AM THE LAW HERE! I AM THE KING...
BA (BWOOSH)
GO (POW)
...HERE—
I SUPPOSE A PIG WHO ONLY KNOWS HOW TO LINE HIS OWN POCKETS...
...CAN'T THINK BEYOND THAT.
SU (SHP)
PIKU (TWITCH)
PIKU
YOU SHOULD LEARN A THING OR TWO ABOUT WHAT IT MEANS TO BE *NORMAL*...
...AND HOW PRECIOUS THAT IS.
PIKU

WHAT? I HAD NO IDEA SOMETHING SO GRAVE WAS OCCURRING IN MY LANDS.
IT SEEMS IT'S ALSO BEEN HAPPENING IN A PART OF RUBENS.
WAS IT INSTINCT THAT LED YOU TO THE HARBOR?
NO, JUST SEVERAL COINCIDENCES LEADING ME THERE.
HA-HA-HA. STILL AN EXPERT IN HUMILITY, I SEE.
...
HM... ALL RIGHT THEN.
HENCEFORTH, SECOND SHALL BE BANNED FROM OUR KINGDOM.
THOSE WHO ENGAGE IN THE MANUFACTURE, SALE, OR USE OF IT SHALL FACE HEAVY PUNISHMENT.
AND SO, BARON CUTHRA...

AS YOU HAVE DISTRIBUTED A DANGEROUS DRUG WITHIN YOUR LANDS OUT OF YOUR OWN SELF-INTEREST...
...AND HAVE ENGAGED IN ACTS THAT MAY HAVE HARMED OTHER NATIONS DUE TO KOHTOKA'S STATUS AS A COMMERCIAL HUB...
...YOU HAVE NO EXCUSE.
YOU WILL FORFEIT YOUR TITLE, LAND, AND FORTUNE.
GAKUN (SLUMP)
TAKE HIM AWAY.
WAIT, NOT YET.
WAS THAT NOT ENOUGH?
HE WAS DEFI-NITELY THE ONE WHO SPREAD THE DRUGS.
BUT WE DON'T KNOW WHO MADE THEM. I'D LIKE TO ASK HIM ABOUT THAT.
I DO KNOW THAT IT'S A DEMONKIN...
A DEMON-KIN?
YEEEK!

HE'S GOING TO KILL ME!
I'M DEAD...
I'M DEAD...
I'M DEAD...
I'M DEAD...
AGHH-HHHH! HE'S GOING TO KILL ME!

mission.
30
R&R TRIP, PART 2

WOW! THERE ARE SO MANY OPTIONS!
MISS PRIMA DONNA, WHICH DESIGN DO YOU LIKE?
NOW THAT WE ARE HERE, IF I MAY ASK...
WHAT IS A "SWIMSUIT"?
HUH? WERE YOU GOING TO BUY ONE WITHOUT KNOWING?
MM-HMM!
R-RIGHT...
THEY'RE CLOTHES THAT YOU CAN GET WET AND THAT ARE EASY TO SWIM IN. DOES THAT MAKE SENSE?
SINCE IT'S HARD TO SWIM IN NORMAL CLOTHES...
WHY NOT SWIM IN THE BUFF?
YOU—
YOU CAN'T DO THAT! THAT'S LEWD! IT'S SCANDALOUS! YOU CAN'T WALK ON THE BEACH LIKE THAT!

'TIS NO MATTER AS LONG AS ONE WAITS TO DISROBE IN THE WATER.
GASHI (GRAB)
THAT'S NOT...
...THE POINT!
GYU (SQUEEZE)
DEEP DOWN, EVERY GIRL...
...WANTS TO WEAR CUTE CLOTHES!
...WHAT A GIRL WANTS!!!
WANTING YOUR CRUSH TO SEE YOU IN A CUTE OUTFIT...
THAT'S ...
BA (SWISH)
BAAAAN (TA-DAAA)

...OH?
IS...
IS THAT WHAT THEY ARE FOR ...?
OH!
ISN'T THIS SWIM-SUIT CUTE!?
YES... YOUR TASTE IS ACCEPT-ABLE.
THIS IS AROUND MY SIZE. YOU MAY FIND SOME POTENTIAL OUTFITS FOR ME.
WHAT!?
YOU'RE MAKING ME CHOOSE FOR YOU!?
WELL...
I SUPPOSE I COULD ...
HMM... WHAT WOULD LOOK GOOD ON YOU...?

I THINK ALL OF THESE WOULD LOOK GOOD ON YOU, ACTUALLY...
PURI (POUT)
PURI
HEH-HEH. INDEED, INDEED. THERE IS NO SUCH THING AS AN OUTFIT THAT DOES NOT.
I'M JEALOUS OF YOUR CONFIDENCE... AND THE LOOKS YOU HAVE TO BACK IT UP.
RIGHT...
MAYBE THIS?
THIS MIGHT WORK!
HUH? MISS PRIMA DONNA?

SHALL I CALL OUT TO HIM?
BUT I MIGHT BE MISTAKEN.
!
I MUST SEE HIS FACE...
BATAN (SHUT)
バタン
GI (TUG)
ギッ
ギッ
GI
IT WON'T BUDGE ...
KYORO
きょろ
きょろ
KYORO (TURN)
HYOKO (POP)
ひょこっ
IT'S EMPTY?
NU (LOOM)
ぬぅ

RILEYLA-SAMA.
PON (PAT)
OH, IT'S YOU, DEY. WHAT ARE YOU DOING HERE?
ROLAND-SAMA ASKED ME TO FIND YOU.
SHALL WE GO HOME?
N—
NO, WE CANNOT! YOU MUST LISTEN, DEY! 'TIS LUTHER...
MY YOUNGER BROTHER IS ALIVE!
...WHAT?
HE ENTERED THROUGH THIS WAY.
LET ME SEE?
WAIT... THOSE BAGS...
ARE YOU SURE? THOUGH, IT IS YOU, RILEYLA-SAMA, SO YOU'D KNOW...
OH MY... THIS IS TERRIBLE. WE NEED TO TELL ROLAND-SAMA.
IF HIS HIGHNESS LUTHER IS POSSIBLY INVOLVED, I MIGHT NOT BE ABLE TO HANDLE THIS...

DO YOU KNOW WHAT IS INSIDE THE BAGS, DEY?
YOU MUST LISTEN CARE-FULLY, RILEYLA-SAMA...
THOSE BAGS ARE—
WHAT DO WE HAVE HERE?
GIII (CREAK)
I THOUGHT I HEARD SOMEONE TALKING. WHAT FAMILIAR FACES.
LUTHER!
I AM SO THANKFUL YOU SURVIVED! SO THE REPORT THAT YOU PERISHED IN BATTLE MUST HAVE BEEN MISTAKEN!
WEREN'T YOU YOURSELF SUPPOSED TO BE DEAD, MY DEAR SISTER?

AS YOU CAN SEE, I AM IN GOOD HEALTH!
OH? I DON'T SENSE ANY OF YOUR MANA...
ARE YOU REALLY MY SISTER?
I LOST IT DUE TO COMPLICATIONS.
SU (SHWIP)
YOUR HIGHNESS... WHAT ARE YOU DOING HERE?
GOU (WHOOM)
...!?

YORO (STAGGER)
GET OUT OF MY SIGHT!
LUTHER!
LET US GO BACK TO HELL! ROJE COMES BACK FROM TIME TO TIME, SO WE CAN RETURN WITH HER...
WHO WOULD GO BACK TO THAT DULL PLACE?
ISN'T THAT ENOUGH?
LET'S GO BACK HOME, RILEYLA-SAMA.
I PREFER IT HERE. I CAN BE MYSELF.
BUT...
PLEASE, JUST FOR NOW.
THE FOOD IS GOOD, AND THERE ARE PLENTY OF FINE WOMEN, BUT MOST IMPORTANTLY...
...NO ONE COMPARES ME TO A GENIUS.
BIKU (JOLT)
SO, CANDICE...

HOW MUCH DO YOU KNOW?
NOTH-ING...
I REALLY DON'T...
OH, COME TO THINK OF IT...
I BELIEVE THE DEMON LORD IS DEAD.
BUT I AM VERY MUCH ALIVE.
?
GU (GRIT)
WHAT DEMON LORD HAS NO MANA?
LET'S GO!
PLEASE, WE NEED TO RUN! QUICKLY!
BUT...
GUI (TUG)
HIS HIGHNESS'S CONTEMPT FOR YOU WAS WELL-KNOWN THROUGHOUT THE ARMY, RILEYLA-SAMA.
VUUUN (WOOM)
IN WHICH CASE, THE PERSON IN FRONT OF ME MUST BE...
IN OTHER WORDS...

YOU MUST BE A THIEF...
...WHO HAS STOLEN THE DEMON LORD'S IDENTITY!
HE INTENDS TO KILL YOU RIGHT NOW!
HMPH...
SO YOU WISH TO FIGHT?
ZA (SHK)
FINALLY, SOME ENTERTAINMENT!
BUWA (FWOOM)
GUN (WHOOM)

ZU (ZOOSH)
GOBU (SPURT)
HAAAH...
HOW BORING. YOU ONLY LASTED A SECOND...

DOMU (WHAM)
DOSA (THUD)
HUH... DEY?
HEY ...
... DEY?

SO... SISTER...
ジャリ...
JARI (CRUNCH)
US MEETING HERE MUST BE FATE...
...OR RATHER, DESTINY.
SO, ACTU-ALLY...
...I ALWAYS HATED YOU.
IT WAS ALWAYS GENIUS THIS, MOST POWERFUL DEMON LORD IN HISTORY THAT!
EVERYONE LAVISHED YOU WITH PRAISE.
BUT WHAT DOES THAT MATTER ...?

NOW THAT YOU'RE IN YOUR CURRENT SITUATION...
...
...YOU'RE JUST A WORTH-LESS WEAK-LING!
BACHI (CRACKLE)
BACHI
BACHI
NOW, DISAP-PEAR...
...FROM MY SIGHT!
GUWA (WHOOM)

GO (THOOM)
IF RILA IS A WEAKLING, THEN YOU MUST BE A NOBODY.

DOGON (KABOOM)
WHAT ARE YOU DOING HERE?
I WAS DOING AN INVESTIGATION. WHEN I WENT THROUGH A GATE ON THE PREMISES, I ENDED UP HERE.
WHAT? OF ALL THE PEOPLE TO SHOW UP...

THAT IS MY YOUNGER BROTHER, LUTHER DIAKITEP.
SO HE WAS A COM-MANDER.
THAT EXPLAINS WHY DEY DIDN'T STAND A CHANCE.
PU (SPIT)
AND IT'S JUST A HUMAN.
I INTENDED TO JUST CAPTURE HIM, BUT I'VE CHANGED MY MIND.
HM?
OH? WHAT COULD THE LIKES OF A HUMAN POSSIBLY DO TO ME?
KILL YOU.
BIKUN (FLINCH)
!
...
WHAT !?

HA! A HUMAN? KILL ME!?
THAT'S RIGHT. YOU'RE A NOBODY WHO'LL DIE AT THE HANDS OF A HUMAN.
TELL ME THIS BEFORE YOU DIE— WHAT IS SECOND? DID YOU MAKE IT?
WHAT'S THE POINT OF KNOWING?
YOU'RE THE ONE WHO'S GONNA END UP DEAD!
JUST KEEP YAPPING AWAY!
BA- (BWOOSH)
I SEE. OH WELL, THEN.
I'LL LOOK INTO IT LATER.

SU (SHF)
UH!?
WHERE DID HE—
ZA (SHK)
ZA
I HEAR THAT'S AN ADVANCED TECHNIQUE...
WHAT WAS IT CALLED AGAIN? MAGI RAEGAS?
TAN
TAN (TMP)

DAMN IT! YOU CAN USE ADVANCED MAGIC!?
ぶ
BUN (BWOOSH)
YOU GIVE ME TOO MUCH CREDIT.
IT'S JUST MY LOSER SKILL.
ん!!
THAT'S NOT ENOUGH.
HE'S LACKING...
EVERYTHING ABOUT HIM IS OVERWHELMINGLY UNDERWHELMING.
HIS EXPERIENCE, TECHNIQUE, APPROACH, STRATEGY...
...AND OF COURSE, HIS POWER TOO.

SUKA (SHWUP)
IT SEEMS YOU'VE ONLY PICKED ON THOSE WEAKER THAN YOURSELF.
BIKI (SNAP)
TAKE THIIIIS!!
BUN (BWOOSH)
BUN
BUN
BUN
THE DEMON LORD DIDN'T ALLOW ME TIME TO CONTEMPLATE TO MYSELF.
BUT RIGHT NOW, I'M EVEN CONVERSING WITH YOU.
DO YOU UNDERSTAND WHAT THAT MEANS?
BALANCING OFFENSE AND DEFENSE IN A BATTLE IS A MATTER OF LIFE AND DEATH.
YOU'RE DEVOTING YOURSELF ONLY TO OFFENSE...
HAAH...
HAAH...
HAAH...
HAAH...

GA (GRAB)
...BUT THAT'S SOME-THING...
GON (THUD)
...I CAN DO TOO!
BACHII (CRACKLE)
!?
HUH...?
HOW?
MAGI RAEGAS REQUIRES PRECISE MANA MANIPULA-TION...
HOW COULD A HUMAN BE CAPABLE OF IT!?
THIS IS THE SAME TECHNIQUE YOU PUT SO MUCH FAITH AND PRIDE INTO.
DON'T UNDER-ESTIMATE HUMANS.
FU (FWIP)
LUTHER...

THIS MAN IS THE ONE WHO DEFEATED ME AND SEALED MY MANA WITH THIS COLLAR.
YOU NEVER STOOD A CHANCE.
SO DO NOT BE DISCOURAGED.
...!
SHUT UP!
WHY ARE YOU ON HIS SIDE!?
EVEN AN EMBARRASSMENT LIKE YOU HAS NO SELF-RESPECT AS A DEMONKIN!?
BACHIN (SLAP)
DON'T YOU DARE TALK ABOUT SELF-RESPECT.
RILA IS TRYING TO HELP HER PEOPLE WHO WERE STRANDED IN THIS LAND AFTER THE CHAOS OF THE WAR.
AND THAT INCLUDES YOU.
GI (GRIT)

NO... YOU MAY BE RIGHT. PERHAPS I HAVE BEEN SHAMELESS.
I FELL IN LOVE WITH THIS MAN...
I KNEW IT.
YOU WEREN'T WORTHY OF BEING OUR RULER. YOU NEVER SHOULD HAVE BECOME OUR DEMON LORD.
IF ONLY I...
IF ONLY I HAD BECOME THE DEMON LORD!
HA!
YOU? THE ONE WHO TRIED TO SELL A DANGER-OUS DRUG IN THE HUMAN WORLD?
HOW WORTHY YOU ARE.
LUTHER, DOES ANY OF IT REALLY MATTER ANYMORE?
WHAT DOES IT MATTER WHO THE DEMON LORD IS OR WHICH RACE IS SUPERIOR TO THE OTHER?

...
... YOU.
SCREW YOU!
SCREW YOU! SCREW YOU! SCREW YOU! SCREW YOU! SCREW YOU! SCREW YOU!
YOU THINK YOU HAVE THE RIGHT TO SAY THAT!?
YOU'RE THE LAST PERSON WHO COULD MAKE THAT CLAIM!
DO YOU KNOW HOW MANY OF OUR OWN...
...WERE UNDONE BY A SINGLE WORD FROM YOU!?
IF YOU WANTED TO PLAY THE VILLAIN, YOU SHOULD HAVE KEPT IT UP TO THE END!
DON'T YOU DARE LOOK AT ME WITH KINDNESS!
IF ONLY THE DEMON LORD...
...HAD BEEN ME...
YOU'RE RIGHT.
I AGREE.

BECAUSE I WAS BURDENED WITH BEING THE MOST POWERFUL DEMON LORD IN HISTORY, THE PRO-WAR FACTION WAS LARGE.
HOWEVER, I NEVER HAD ANY INTEREST IN WHICH RACE WAS SUPERIOR TO THE OTHER AND SIMPLY GAVE NONCOMMITTAL EXCUSES TO PREVENT IT.
BUT AT A CERTAIN POINT, I REACHED MY LIMIT.
IF I HAD DONE NOTHING, OUR NATION LIKELY WOULD HAVE BEEN BECOME DIVIDED.
THE WAR WAS JUST ANOTHER POLITICAL DECISION.
TO BEAR SUCH A BURDEN IS SIMPLY ANOTHER DUTY OF THE DEMON LORD.
SO THE RESPONSIBILITY FOR THAT LIES WITH ME AS WELL.
HOWEVER, DESPITE THAT, I STILL BELIEVE I UPHELD MY OWN IDEALS AND BELIEFS.
HOWEVER, NO MATTER HOW I TRIED...
...IT STILL EXHAUSTED ME...
AND AT THAT TIME, THIS MAN I MET GAVE ME THE OPPORTUNITY...
...TO LEAVE MY ROLE AS THE DEMON LORD BEHIND.

WHAT THE HELL...? DAMN IT.
HOW POWERFUL ARE YOU?
YOU DEFEATED A PRODIGY AND EVEN CHANGED HER VERY NATURE?
UGH, DAMN IT!
DOSA (THUD)
WHAT A LOAD OF CRAP.
IT REALLY WAS.
THE PARTS WE BOTH HAD TO PLAY WERE CRAP.

RILA, DEMONKIN ARE CAPABLE OF NECRO-MANCY, AREN'T THEY?
YES, HOWEVER, 'TIS FORBIDDEN MAGIC IN HELL.
I DON'T CARE. THIS ISN'T HELL.
MUMU (POUT)
ムゥッ

LISTEN HERE! IT IS FORBIDDEN DUE TO THE OVERWHELMING BURDEN IT PLACES UPON THE CASTER.
AND AS FOR HOW THAT WORKS, WELL...
TO PUT IT SIMPLY, THE MAGIC TRANSFERS PART OF ONE'S LIFE FORCE...
IT INDISPUTABLY FALLS INTO COURT-RANK MONO MAGIC!
I DON'T CARE ABOUT THE THEORY. I'M GOING TO BRING BACK DEY.
I AM TELLING YOU THAT IF THIS GOES AWRY, EVEN I CANNOT IMAGINE WHAT WILL HAPPEN!
YOU MAY EVEN PERISH.
I ATTEMPTED IT ONLY ONCE IN MY YOUTH...
I DON'T CARE HOW RISKY IT IS. I CAN'T LET HER DIE LIKE THIS.
HMPH... IF YOU PUT IT THAT WAY, I SUPPOSE I REALLY CANNOT SAY NO TO YOU...

THEN I SHALL MAKE SURE YOU SUCCEED!
I THINK WE SHOULD BE FAR ENOUGH FROM PRYING EYES HERE.

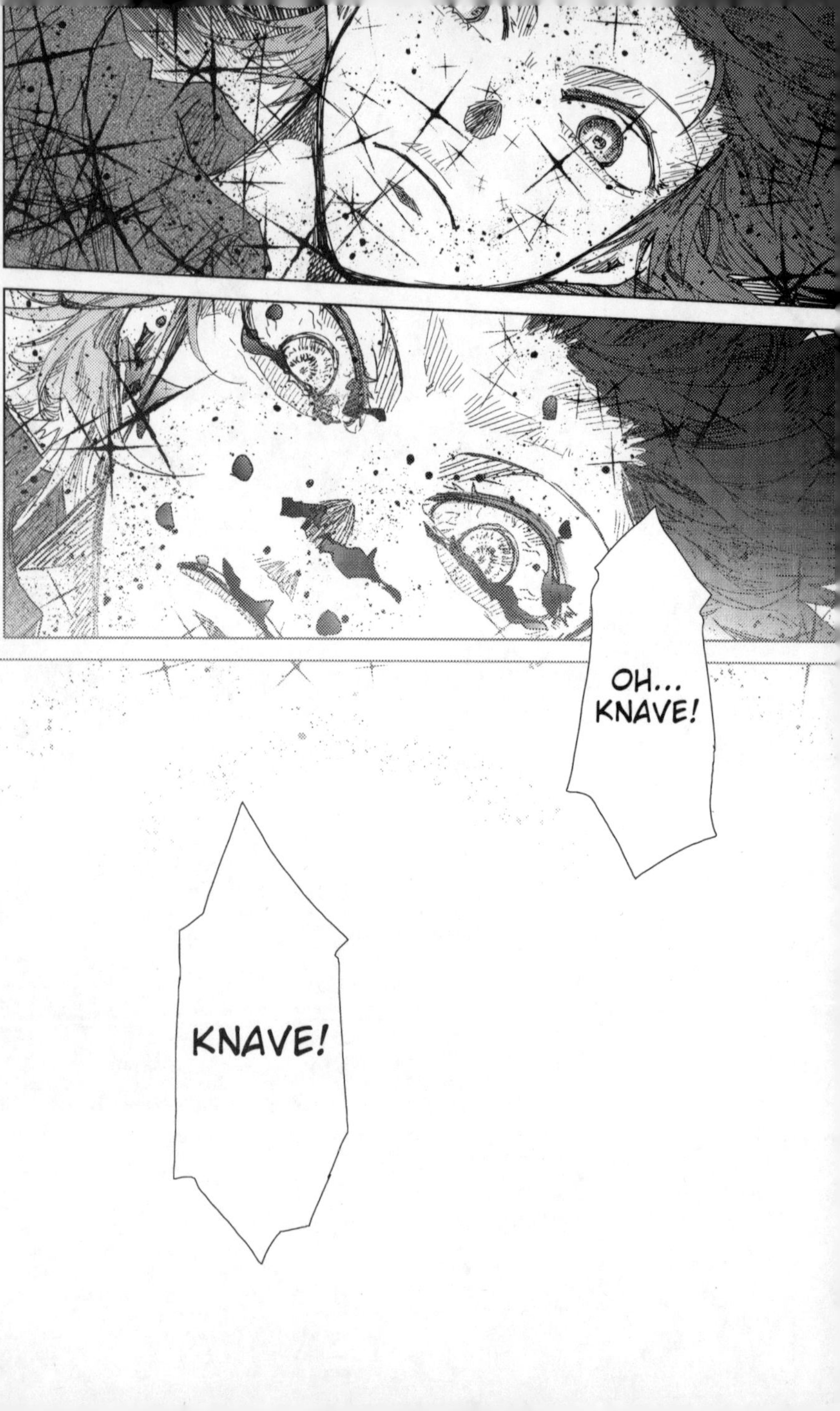
OH... KNAVE!
KNAVE!

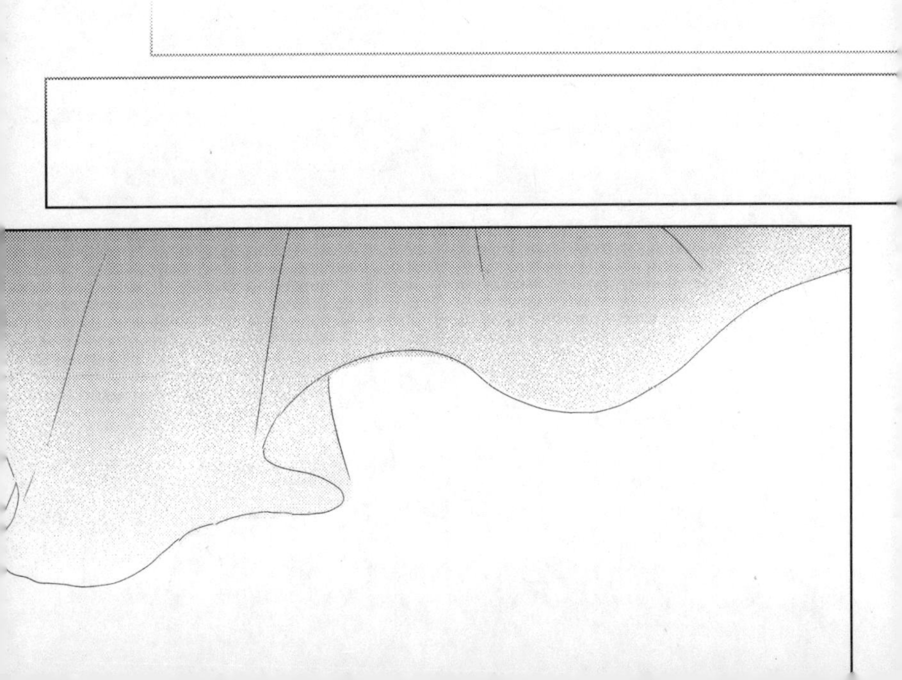

...
ぐいっ
GUI (STRETCH)
mission. 31
R&R TRIP, PART 3
MY BODY FEELS HEAVY.
ZUUUN (SLUNK)
ず———ん…

OF COURSE YOU DO! YOU USED COURT-RANK MONO NECRO-MANCY ON A VAMPIRE!
IT'S ALREADY BEEN TWO DAYS.
YES, ONLY TWO! 'TIS A MIRACLE YOU CAN EVEN MOVE!
I LOST CONSCIOUS-NESS FOR SEVERAL HOURS BACK THEN.
HOURS... THAT'S IM-PRESSIVE.
THE RECOIL DEPENDS UPON THE SPELL'S TARGET.
RIGHT, YOU DID SAY YOU USED NECROMANCY ONCE BEFORE.
YES, THAT WAS ON ORETEN-BERG.
WHO IS THAT?
THE CAT I USED TO HAVE ...
COME NOW! THAT IS ENOUGH CHITCHAT. YOU SHOULD REST A BIT MORE!
THERE'S NOTHING HINDERING ME FROM EVERYDAY ACTIVITIES.
YOU ARE NOT INFALLIBLE. YOU MUST TAKE CARE OF YOURSELF FROM TIME TO TIME.
GUI (NUDGE)
GUI

WE STILL DON'T KNOW WHERE THE SECOND CAME FROM.
'TIS A TYPE OF ANALGESIC FROM HELL.
THE STUFF WE FOUND IN THE WAREHOUSE WAS A POWDER. WASN'T HELL USING A LIQUID?
I AM SURPRISED YOU WERE AWARE OF THAT.
POWDERED MEDICINE WAS POPULAR PRIOR TO THE WAR.
HOWEVER, ON THE FRONTLINES, IT WAS DIFFICULT TO USE.
BECAUSE OF THAT, WE DEVELOPED A LIQUID THAT ALL TROOPS ADOPTED.
I ENTRUSTED MANAGEMENT OF THE WAREHOUSE TO SOMEONE, SO I DO NOT KNOW WHAT BECAME OF IT.
AS A RESULT, A LARGE STOCK OF POWDERED MEDICINE LIKELY REMAINED.
HOWEVER, THE MEDICINE IS HARMLESS TO DEMONKIN.
SO IT SEEMS TO HAVE UNEXPECTED SIDE EFFECTS ON HUMANS, THEN.
JUST WHERE IN THE WORLD DID HE LEARN THAT SILLY BIT OF TRIVIA?
OH, THAT FOOL...
HAH...

KON
KON (KNOCK)
GACHARI (CHK)
ROLAND-SAMA?
YOU CAN GET UP NOW?
YES.
THOUGH I'M NOT BATTLE-READY JUST YET.
HOW ARE YOU?
HEE-HEE-HEE. ♥ AS YOU CAN SEE, I'M DOING GREAT...
...ALL THANKS TO YOU!
THOUGH MY CHEST FEELS A BIT BREEZY.
IT'S FINE, I'LL JUST STICK AN APPLE IN THE HOLE.

BEING BOTH AN IMMORTAL VAMPIRE AND UNDEAD SEEMS LIKE A CONTRADICTION.
IT'S NOT THAT INCONVENIENT THOUGH.
IT'S ACTUALLY A LITTLE CONVENIENT, SINCE I NO LONGER FEEL THE NEED TO DRINK BLOOD.
ANYWAY, IT LOOKS LIKE YOU'RE FINE.
?
LET'S HURRY UP AND GO, THEN. EVERYONE IS WAITING.
WHAT DO YOU MEAN?
HUH ...?
RILEYLA-SAMA, DID YOU NOT TELL HIM?
OH, UM... I COULDN'T FIND A GOOD MOMENT ...
OH MY, THAT AGAIN? YOU'RE STILL AVOIDING IT? JUST ACCEPT IT.
IT'S NOT SO SIMPLE.
YOU'RE SO BASHFUL ABOUT THE WEIRDEST THINGS.
WHERE ARE WE GOING?
I WOULD SAY IT'S ODDER THAT YOU ARE NOT BASHFUL!
THAT'S OBVIOUS, SINCE WE'RE AT A HARBOR.

NGHHH!
I SIMPLY DO NOT HAVE THE NERVE TO WEAR ONLY THIS SMALL SCRAP OF FABRIC!
WHY CAN I NOT SIMPLY SWIM IN THE NUDE!?
ZAPAAAN (ZWSHHH)
THAT WOULD BE EVEN MORE SCANDALOUS, RILA-CHAN.

OH! ROLAND-SAAAN!
I'M NOT SURE I UNDERSTAND WHY YOU FEEL THAT WAY...
JUST THINK OF IT AS EQUIPMENT FOR THE WATER, RILEYLA-SAMA.
YES?

THANKS FOR WAITING!
IT TOOK A LONG TIME TO COAX RILEYLA-SAMA TO COME WITH US.
WHO WOULD WILLINGLY WEAR SUCH AN OUTFIT!?
I'M GLAD YOU'RE FEELING BETTER.
I'M SORRY FOR WORRYING YOU.
WELL...
I BELIEVED YOU WOULD BE FINE.
WHAT?
YOU WERE SUPER-WORRIED TOO THOUGH, BRANCH MANAGER!
SH-
SHUSH!
MORE IMPORTANTLY, IF YOU DRESS LIKE THAT, YOU'LL END UP SUNBURNED!
ISN'T IT NORMAL TO GET TAN AT THE BEACH?
Y-
YOU'LL REGRET THAT IN A DECADE!
WHAT ARE YOU DOING, KNAVE?
...
I'M GOING TO SWIM TO THE ISLAND OVER THERE.
AN ISLAND?
WHAT? THAT'S SO FAR AWAY! WHY WOULD YOU DO THAT!?
ESPECIALLY WHEN WE'RE AT THE BEACH?
OH DEAR, MY OH MY.
YES, IT'S ESPECIALLY BECAUSE WE'RE AT THE BEACH.

HMPH!!
THEN I SUPPOSE WE SHOULD HAVE FUN OURSELVES AS WELL ...
BUT ONLY THOSE OF US IN OUR SWIMSUITS.
OH, SHE'S RIGHT.
IT'S NOT AS THOUGH SHE CAN DO MUCH BUNDLED UP IN THAT TOWEL.
MU (POUT)
MU
MU
YEAH, LET'S GO AHEAD!
LET'S GO!
MU
MU
MU
BA (BWIP)
I SUPPOSE SACRI-FICES MUST BE MADE!
I SHALL JOIN IN YOUR FESTIVI-TIES!
BASHA (SPLASH)
BASHA

HAAH. THAT SURE WAS TIRING.
INDEED... BUT THIS SWIMSUIT IS NOT SO BAD.
WHERE ARE THE OTHERS?
THEY WENT TO PREP THE BARBECUE.
ZAWA (CLAMOR)
ザワ
WAI (CHATTER)
ワイ
ZAWA
WAI
WHAT HAPPENED?
APPARENTLY, AN ELF WASHED UP ON SHORE.
ZAWA
WAI
OUT OF THE WAY! OUTTA THE WAY!

IS THAT ROJE?
SEEMS LIKE IT.
I THOUGHT SHE WAS A DARK ELF?
NO, THAT IS SIMPLY HER DISGUISE.
SHE LOATHES TO BE UNDER-ESTIMATED AND SO PRETENDS TO BE A DARK ELF.
...
PERHAPS DROWNING DRAINED HER OF HER MANA?
BUT WHY CROSS THE OCEAN TO GET HERE?
DOES SHE LIVE OUT THERE?
NO, SHE RESIDES IN HELL.
PIIIPOOO
PIIIPOOO (WEEWOO)
PAKA
PAKA (CLOP)
THEN IT MUST BE ANOTHER ELF.
SHE HAS NO REASON TO BE HERE, AFTER ALL.
EVERYONE, WE'RE READY!

ROLAND-SAN, TODAY...
...ARE YOU PLANNING TO GO OUT WITH MISS PRIMA DONNA?
NO, SHE LEFT TO GO SHOPPING.
YESSSSSs!!
HERE ARE SHOP PAMPHLETS.
YOU HAVE YOUR PICK OF ANY PLACE!
A MOST EXCELLENT JOB YOU HAVE DONE!
SHOWING HER TONS OF SHOPS PAID OFF!
NYAFU (CACKLE)
FUNSU (PUFF)
YES! YES! YES! MILIA, YOU DID IT! YOU DID IT!
NYAFUFU
OH!

AHEM!
I-IN THAT CASE...
...WOULD YOU COME LOOK AROUND THE TOWN WITH ME?
I WOULDN'T MIND.
YAY!
I-I-I-IN THAT CASE!
LET'S MEET AT THE ENTRANCE IN HALF AN HOUR!
ALL RIGHT.
YES! YES! YES!!!
BATAN (SHUT)
HOW MUCH MONEY DID I HAVE AGAIN?
I'M SOMEWHAT WORRIED SINCE I HADN'T PLANNED TO STAY SO LONG.
TON (KNOCK)
TON
I'M COM-ING IN!

DID SOMETHING HAPPEN?
HMM?
DO I NEED A REASON TO VISIT YOU?
I HEARD FROM RILEYLA-SAMA THAT YOU'RE STAYING HERE A BIT LONGER.
I PLAN ON GOING HOME TOMORROW.
THEN DO YOU HAVE TIME THIS AFTERNOON?
THIS AFTERNOON?
I GUESS I DO.
OH, GOODY! THEN COME MEET ME AT THE ROCKS NEAR THE BEACH.
GYUU (SQUEEZE)
LET'S HAVE ... ...A GOOD TIME?
WHAT DOES THAT MEAN?
HEE HEE.
YOU'LL JUST NEED TO COME AND FIND OUT. ♥
ALL RIGHT.

HIRA HIRA
HIRA (FLIT)
HEE-HEE. I'LL BE WAITING.
GII (KREE)
WELL, I SHOULD BE DONE WITH THE WALK AROUND TOWN BY THEN.
I SHOULD GET READY SOON.
TON (KNOCK)
TON
DO YOU HAVE A MOMENT?
BRANCH MANAGER? COME IN.
GACHARI (CHK)
I'M SORRY FOR COMING BY SO EARLY IN THE MORNING. I WONDERED IF TODAY—

HM?
ARE YOU GOING OUT?
YES.
MILIA-SAN ASKED ME TO JOIN HER.
HM...
HRMM...
ふる
FURU
ふる
FURU (QUIVER)
THAT GIRL! I DIDN'T EXPECT HER TO MAKE PLANS WITH HIM SO EARLY IN THE MORNING!
THANK YOU FOR YESTERDAY.
IT WAS A GOOD CHANGE OF PACE.
W—
WAS IT? GOOD!
RILA AND CANDEY-SAN ALSO HAD A GREAT TIME.
HAAH...
WELL, IT SEEMS YOU'RE SUR-ROUNDED BY BEAUTIFUL WOMEN AROUND THE CLOCK.
WHAT A DECEITFUL MAN YOU ARE. THAT'S JUST WHAT MAKES YOU OUR ACE EMPLOYEE.
YOUR... ACE?
BUT DON'T PUSH YOURSELF TOO FAR. YOU'RE STILL RECUPERAT-ING, AFTER ALL.
I'LL BE CAREFUL.

OH...
I HEARD THE STAFF WHO WENT HOME AHEAD OF US ARRIVED FINE.
I WAS HOPING FOR ANOTHER DAY OFF FOR ONCE, THOUGH.
OH WELL. I'LL GO TAKE A TOUR AROUND AS PART OF MY DUTIES FOR THE BRANCH.
SEE YOU.
KA KA (CLACK)
GACHI (SHAKE)
S-S-S-S!
D— SORRY FOR MAKING YOU WAIT!
DID YOU HAVE TO WAIT LONG!?
GACHI
GACHI
NO, NOT AT ALL.
OH— UH—
GOOD!

I-IT'S ALMOST LIKE A DATE! THIS IS SO NICE!
LET'S GET GOING!
APPARENTLY, THE STORES IN THIS AREA SELL A LOT OF RARE SUNDRIES FROM ALL KINDS OF OTHER COUNTRIES.
I LIKE THINGS LIKE THIS, SO I'M EXCITED JUST TO EVEN SEE WHAT THEY HAVE!
I SEE... I WONDERED WHAT HER AIM COULD BE ASKING ME TO SIMPLY LOOK AROUND TOWN...
...BUT THIS IS INDEED QUITE INTER-ESTING.
SIR, I'D LIKE ONE OF THESE.

HAAAH!
THAT WAS SUCH A TREAT FOR THE EYES! ♪
HOW ABOUT LUNCH AT THE USUAL CAFÉ?
OH, RIGHT... IT'S ALREADY AFTERNOON. WHAT SHOULD WE EAT?
AFTERNOON...
OH!
THAT SEAFOOD PLACE IS POPULAR!
THE SHRIMP DISHES LOOK GOOD.
I'LL GO USE THE RESTROOM, SO PLEASE FIND A SEAT FOR US.
ALL RIGHT. I WILL! ♪
... ALL RIGHT. LET'S GO.
BAN (SLAM)
DEY IS PROBABLY ALREADY THERE BY NOW.
DA
DA (DASH)
DA
DA
SHE'LL LIKELY PRESS ME ON WHY I'M LATE...
BUT...
ZA (ZSSH)
ZA

I JUST NEED TO MAKE HER THINK I'M NOT LATE!
HAAAH...
I WONDER IF ROLAND-SAMA IS HERE YET.
?
HEY, WHAT ARE YOU MUTTERING ABOUT?
TA (TMP)
HUH...OH. COME ON! YOU'RE LATE. WHAT WERE YOU—
I WAS ALREADY HERE. YOU JUST DIDN'T NOTICE ME.
THEN YOU COULD HAVE SAID SOMETHING EARLIER.
CHAPU
CHAPU (SPLISH)
IS THAT YOUR SURPRISE FOR ME? LET'S GET IT OVER WITH.
OH, DON'T BE IN SUCH A RUSH. ♥
HEE HEE...

BISHI (BWISHT)
ZA (ZSH)
ZA
YOU HAVE ONLY ONE FISHING ROD AND ALREADY HAVE A HOLDER FOR IT.
DOES THIS REALLY REQUIRE TWO PEOPLE?
OF COURSE IT DOES... BECAUSE ...
...WE CAN HAVE SOME FUN WHILE WE WAIT, CAN'T WE?
NO, I DON'T HAVE TIME TO DO THIS TODAY.
MMMM!♥

BASHAN (SPLASH)
WE GOT ONE.
HUH!?
YOU HANDLE THE ROD.
WHAT!?
WHAAAAAA!?
BA (BWOOSH)
ROLAND-SAMA, YOU DO KNOW HOW FISHING WORKS, RIGHT!?
ZAPAAAN (SPLOOSH)
GOBO (GLUP)
BO
BO
BO

GOBO
PO
PO
PO
PO
PO
PO
PO (PLIP)
GU
GU
GU
GU (FLEX)
OH MY, OH MY!
GUI (TUG)
THIS FEELS LIKE... SOMETHING HUGE!
GU
GU
GU
BUT...
...IT FEELS DIFFERENT FROM EARLIER...
BASHAA (SPLASH)
BASHA
SHA
GU
GU
GU
GU
GU
I KNOW! IT ALMOST FEELS LIKE...
...A WHOLE BUNCH OF CREATURES ARE TUGGING ON THE LINE...
THAT'S HOW THIS FEELS!
WASSE
WASSE
WASSE (HOIST)

EEK!
AHH!
BACHA (SPLISH)
I'M SORRY FOR THE WAIT.
OH... IT'S OKAY! ACTUALLY, ARE YOU ALL RIGHT? I WAS WORRIED YOUR STOMACH WAS...
BOTA (DRIP)
YEEEEEK!?
YOU'RE SOAKING WET!
YES, THE STOMACH PAIN HAD ME SWEATING BUCKETS.
UHH... THAT'S SWEAT!?
SO YOU REALLY AREN'T BETTER YET...
BOTA
BOTA
BOTA
I FEEL BETTER AFTER GOING TO THE RESTROOM, SO IT'S FINE.
LET'S EAT.
HERE'S A WET TOWEL.
THANK YOU.

THEY HAD A GOOD LUNCH SPECIAL, SO I ORDERED THAT.
THANK YOU.
KUI (TUG)
KUI
MESO (SOB)
BORO (TATTERS)
MESO
BORO
UGH...
WHAT WEAK-LINGS...!
HUH?

I MEAN... WHAT A WEAK STOMACH I HAVE... HOW REGRET-TABLE...
UH-HUH!...
EXCUSE ME. I'M AFRAID I NEED TO GO AGAIN.
GATAN (CLATTER)
UH... WOULD YOU LIKE ME TO BUY SOME MEDICINE FOR YOU?
YOU DON'T NEED TO WORRY ABOUT SOMEONE AS HOPELESS AS ME. I'LL GO AND BUY SOME MYSELF.
BATAN (SLAM)
SIR, ONE OF THESE, PLEASE!
THANKS! COME AGAIN!
GI (CRIK)
HAAH...
HAAH...
GI

HAAH...
HOW STRONG IS THIS THING!?
HAAH...
AND HOW LONG WILL THIS BATTLE CONTINUE!?
HAAH...
HAAH...
GU (FLEX)
BUT IT'S MUCH WEAKER THAN BEFORE! JUST A LITTLE MORE!
BACHA
BACHA (SPLISH)
BACHA
...?
GU GU GU
IS ROLAND-SAMA REALLY ALL RIGHT NOT COMING UP TO BREATHE?
!
BASHAAAA (SPLOOOSH)
SHUBO (SHWOOOO)
BO
BO
BO

OH MY, OH MY! WHAT A BIG CATCH!
BUT IT SEEMS TO ALREADY BE DEAD...
AND IT'S COLD, AS THOUGH IT WAS SITTING ON TOP OF ICE...
ITS EYES ARE CLOUDED TOO...
IT ALMOST LOOKS LIKE ONE OF THE FISH AT THE MARKET.
DEY.
THIS WAS THE RESULT OF YOUR BATTLE WITH IT.
YOU MEAN... IT RAN OUT OF STRENGTH?
YES... IT WAS A LONG FIGHT, AFTER ALL.
ZAPAAAN (SPLISH)

THEN LET'S HAVE THIS FOR DINNER!
UPSY-DAISY!
SORRY, BUT I HAVE PLANS AFTER THIS.
I ONLY PROMISED TO GO FISHING WITH YOU.
AW, I GUESS SO...
I'LL MAKE UP FOR IT LATER.
UGH!
REALLY, ROLAND-SAMA!?
UM... IS YOUR STOMACH BETTER?
YOU DIDN'T FORCE YOURSELF TO GO OUT BECAUSE OF ME ...?
I'M FULLY RECOVERED, SO THERE'S NO NEED TO WORRY.
WELL, THAT'S GOOD THEN, BUT... THERE'S THAT...
UM... YOU SEEM TO HAVE SEAWEED ON YOUR HEAD...
びたんっっ!
BITAN (SPLAT)
IT WAS JUST SOME DUST.
RIGHT... DUST...

LUNCH WAS SO GOOD.
I'M SORRY FOR RUINING THINGS.
OH NO! I'M JUST GLAD YOU'RE FEELING BETTER!
A— ALSO...
R— ROLAND-SAN, UM...
AFTER THIS...
...WOULD YOU BE WILLING TO—
I'M SORRY, I HAVE PLANS TONIGHT.
WHA—!?
OH! OF COURSE YOU WOULD!
ESPECIALLY SINCE YOU'RE NOT FEELING FULLY YOURSELF YET...

BUT I'LL TREAT YOU TO ANOTHER MEAL LATER.
WE'LL DO IT ONCE I'M FULLY RECOVERED.
YES! I'M LOOKING FORWARD TO THAT!
WALKING ALONE, ARE WE? HOW LONESOME YOU MUST BE.

YOU LOOK LONE-SOME YOUR-SELF.
HA HA! ♪
YOU ARE GREATLY MISTAKEN! I AM ENJOYING MY TIME TO MYSELF.
RIGHT.
TAKE THIS IF YOU WANT IT.
HUH? IS THIS... FOR ME?
IF YOU DON'T LIKE IT, I CAN RETURN IT.
I'LL USE IT!
I'LL TAKE GOOD CARE OF IT!
SHA (SNATCH)

NNYAAAN (MROWR)
DOESN'T IT LOOK WONDERFUL ON ME?
YEAH.
BISHII (SHWIP)
HA HA HA!
I AM IN SUCH A PLEASANT MOOD!
SO I SHALL SPARE YOU FROM EXPLAINING WHY THIS HAIR BAND IS SOPPING WET.
I'M GLAD TO HEAR THAT.
AH, YES! IT SEEMS YOU ARE ALONE...
...SO I PRESUME YOU DO NOT HAVE PLANS FOLLOWING THIS.
OH, THAT PLACE IS BACK THAT WAY A LITTLE—
NO, THIS WAY!
IN THAT CASE, I SHALL SHOW MY GRATITUDE FOR THIS CAT ACCESSORY BY TREATING YOU TO DINNER.
I HAVE FOUND A WONDERFUL SEAFOOD PLACE. IT SEEMS TO HAVE DELECTABLE SHRIMP.
GUI (TUG)

IS IT FAR?
INDEED. WE WILL NEED TO WALK IN EACH OTHER'S COMPANY FOR SOME TIME.
AT THE HOS-PITAL...
HAAH...
I— I WAITED, BUT YOU NEVER CAME HOME... THOUGHT YOU... ELOPED...
NGH. NGH...
HAAAAAH...
AND ASKED AROUND... FINALLY GOT HERE... BUT WHERE ARE YOU...?
HAAH...
THAT ELF HAS BEEN MUTTERING TO HERSELF THE WHOLE TIME... IT SEEMS LIKE SHE WAS ABANDONED...
AW, POOR THING...

SLATHER ON SUNSCREEN, JUST IN CASE.

UKKI
UKKI (BEAM)
うっき うっき
YOU'LL CATCH A COLD...
I DO NOT WISH TO TAKE IT OFF YET! I SHALL SLEEP IN THIS!
WAKKU (GLEE)
わっく
WAKKU
わっく
ふふーん♪
FUFUUUN (HUM)

mission.
32
REUNION

I HADN'T NOTICED AT THE BEACH...
...BUT IT SEEMS EVEN YOU HAVE SUFFERED SCARS.
OF COURSE I HAVE.
ONLY THIS ONE?
I HAVE OTHERS.

OH, 'TIS TRUE.
YOU HAVE SEVERAL UPON YOUR BACK.
HOW-EVER...
...YOU ONLY HAVE ONE SCAR UPON YOUR CHEST.
WHY IS THAT?
...
IT'S NOT AN INTER-ESTING STORY.
I WAS JUST STILL GREEN, THAT'S ALL.
OH!
GORON (ROLL)

SIR!
COULD I GET A QUEST?
D-RANK ADVENTURER SASHA GLIDEAU
AS YOU WISH.
I'LL TAKE YOUR ADVENTURER PERMIT, THEN.

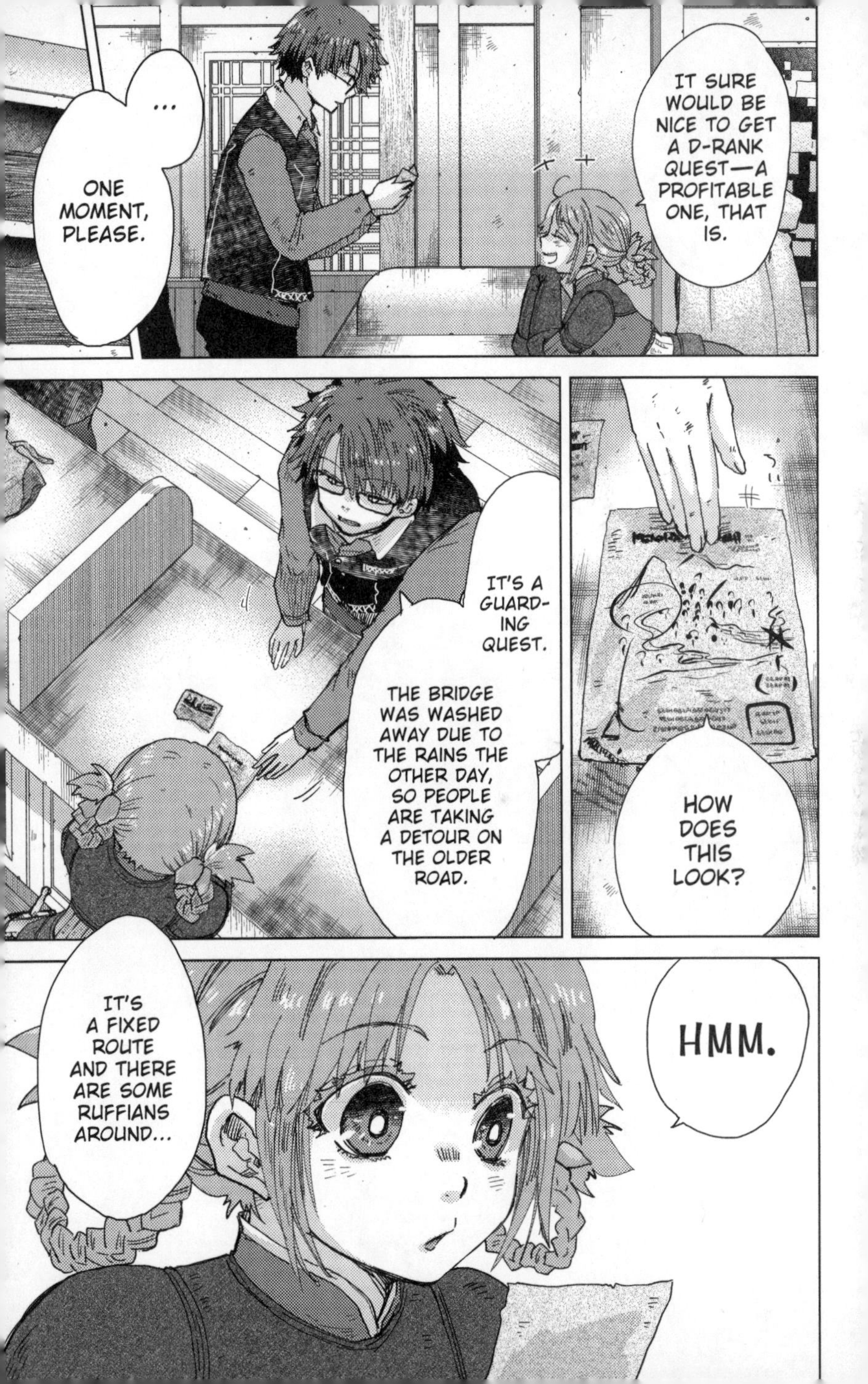
IT SURE WOULD BE NICE TO GET A D-RANK QUEST—A PROFITABLE ONE, THAT IS.
...
ONE MOMENT, PLEASE.
HOW DOES THIS LOOK?
IT'S A GUARDING QUEST.
THE BRIDGE WAS WASHED AWAY DUE TO THE RAINS THE OTHER DAY, SO PEOPLE ARE TAKING A DETOUR ON THE OLDER ROAD.
HMM.
IT'S A FIXED ROUTE AND THERE ARE SOME RUFFIANS AROUND...

SO I JUST NEED TO PROTECT ANYONE PASSING THROUGH?
YES, IF THEY RUN INTO AN EMERGENCY.
OTHER GUILDS HAVE RECEIVED THE SAME QUEST...
...SO SEVERAL PEOPLE WILL HAVE THE SAME JOB, AND YOU'LL DIVVY UP THE LABOR ON SITE.
ALL RIGHT. IT LOOKS LIKE YOU'RE RECRUITING FOR A WHILE TOO.
UNTIL THE BRIDGE IS REPAIRED.
GOT IT.
THEN I'LL TRY IT TODAY AND MIGHT TAKE THE QUEST AGAIN IF IT GOES WELL.
ALL RIGHT. THANK YOU FOR YOUR ASSISTANCE.

DO
DO
DO (THUD)
DO
E-EMER-GENCY!
BATA
BATA (PATTER)
BATA
BATA
A GIGANTIC GEHT-HAWK APPEARED ON THE OLD ROAD!
THE ADVEN-TURERS ON THE SCENE CAN'T HANDLE IT!
PLEASE MAKE AN EMERGENCY QUEST UNDER BARDEL-SAMA'S AUTHORITY AS LORD!

MAKE A QUEST STUB RIGHT AWAY!
WHAT ABOUT THE REWARD!? AND WE NEED CONFIRMA-TION!
YOU THINK WE HAVE TIME TO CHECK IN WITH THE LORD!?
WHAT RANK? B! IT'S B!
SEARCH THE GUILD!
IT'S AN EMERGENCY QUEST! WE NEED A B-RANKER! SOMEONE WE CAN GET IN TOUCH WITH NOW!
SHIN (HUSH)
DAMN IT! THIS IS BAD TIMING!
JUST SEND A REQUEST TO THE OTHER GUILDS AS A LAST RESORT!
GET AHOLD OF YOUR-SELVES!

BRANCH MANAGER IRIS!
ROLAND, CAN I COUNT ON YOU?
THE STATE OF THE ADVEN-TURERS GUILD...
...ISN'T NEARLY AS IMPORTANT AS THE SAFETY OF THOSE ON THE SCENE.
ALL RIGHT.

I'LL BORROW YOUR HORSE.
GIVE ME A BRIEF SUMMARY OF WHAT YOU KNOW.
Y-YES, SIR.
HUH!? WAIT A SECOND!
YOU CAN'T GO EMPTY-HANDED!
I NEED ONLY MYSELF.
PO (BLUSH)
HE'S SO COOL...
PO
PO
PO

YOU ONLY HAVE ONE SCAR UPON YOUR CHEST.

A GEHT-HAWK... A DANGEROUS MAN-EATING MONSTER BIRD THAT PRIMARILY LIVES IN THE MOUNTAINS.
THE OLD ROAD GOES THROUGH SUCH TERRAIN.
I WOULDN'T BE SURPRISED THAT THEY ENCOUNTERED ONE.
BUT BECAUSE NO ONE HAD WITNESSED IT, WE HADN'T FACTORED IT INTO THE PLAN...
IF IT'S LARGE, IT'D BE ABLE TO SWALLOW A WHOLE PERSON IN ONE GULP.
HEL...
HELP ME...

THIS GIANT BIRD SUDDENLY APPEARED. WHAT IS THAT THING!?
WE CAN'T DO IT! WE DON'T HAVE A CHANCE IN HELL AGAINST IT...
DO YOU KNOW AN ADVENTURER NAMED SASHA?
SASHA?
WAIT, YOU'RE A GUILD EMPLOYEE?
OH! YOU MEAN THAT GIRL, THE D-RANKER...
SHE'S BACK THERE!
SHE SAID SHE COULD MANAGE IT...
GOT IT!
HEY! YOU CAN'T TAKE IT ON ALONE! CALL FOR HELP!

KIIIIIEEEEE (SKREEEEE)
BASAAAAAA (FLAP)
BASA
KIIIII
BASA
KIRI (SHNK)
BASA
GU (TUG)
JUST GO AWAY ALREADY!
PYUN
PYUN (FWISH)
PYUN
PYUN

GIRORI (GLARE)
BIKUN (FLINCH)
WAAAAAAAH!?
AAAAAA (CAAAAW)
STAY DOWN.
THE STAFFER!?
HUH?

KURU (TURN)
BASSA (FLAP)
SA (SHF)
BYUWA (BWOOSH)
BASSA
BASSA
BASSA
DO (THUNK)

STAFF-ER!
DOSA (STAB)
THANK YOU...
DON'T, IT WAS AN EMERGENCY.
I THOUGHT IT WAS JUST A MEASLY GEHT-HAWK, BUT...
...I DIDN'T THINK IT'D BE THAT BIG.
HUH?
UM, YOUR...
YES, THOSE WEREN'T EXPENSIVE.

THIS IS THE SECOND TIME, ISN'T IT? THAT YOU'VE SAVED ME?
THAT'S RIGHT! IT IS!
I DIDN'T NOTICE SINCE YOU HAD YOUR GLASSES ON BEFORE.
NO, IT'S THE FIRST TIME. YOU MUST HAVE ME MISTAKEN FOR SOME-ONE ELSE.
HUH?
I'LL RETURN TO THE GUILD AND MAKE MY REPORT.
PLEASE COME BACK WITH THE AID UNIT THAT'S COMING.

SO SHE REMEM-BERED ME.

YOU CAN'T GO EMPTY-HANDED!
I NEED ONLY MYSELF. (GLINT!)
SERIOUSLY! HE IS SOOO COOL!
KYAAA (SQUEEE)
きゃ
PEOPLE SEEM TO REALLY LIKE YOU, ARGAN-SAN.

ALL THE ADVENTURERS I'VE MET IN THIS TOWN SAY THE SAME THING.
THEY SAY YOU'RE AN AMAZING STAFFER, SO I CAN'T GO WRONG GETTING A QUEST FROM YOU.
IS THAT SO? WHAT AN HONOR.
THAT SURE DIDN'T SOUND VERY GENUINE.
BOO!
I'M AFRAID I DON'T HAVE PROFITABLE D-RANK QUESTS TODAY.
THEN ARE THERE ANY IN OTHER RANKS I COULD DO?
YES, WELL, THERE'S AN E-RANK ONE...
HOW WOULD YOU FEEL ABOUT AN HERB-GATHERING QUEST FOR *KONSOU*, WHICH IS USED TO MAKE HEALING POTIONS?
...
I THOUGHT SO.

YOUR VIBE IS TOTALLY DIFFERENT WITH THOSE GLASSES ON.
HEY, WHY ARE YOU LYING? I'M PRETTY SURE YOUR VISION ISN'T IMPAIRED.
I'M NOT LYING.
THESE ARE...
...A FASHION STATEMENT.
AH HA HA!
THEY'RE A FASHION WHAT?
ZUI (SHHF)
ズイ
FINE.
I'LL TAKE IT.
THAT HERB QUEST.
AS YOU WISH.
IF YOU RUN INTO AN UNEXPECTED FOE LIKE LAST TIME, PLEASE RUN AWAY.
I GOT IT, I GOT IT.

I'M STILL IN RANK D, EVEN IF I DON'T LOOK IT, YOU KNOW. ARE YOU JUST A WORRY-WART?
I ONLY GIVE THE APPROPRIATE AMOUNT OF WORRY TO THOSE WHO SEEM RASH OR LIKELY TO MAKE A MISTAKE.
HEY, THAT'S MEAN!
IS THAT HOW I SEEM TO YOU?
I'M SORRY, BUT...
...THERE ARE PEOPLE BEHIND YOU.
AH!?
ZORO
ZORO (SHUFFLE)
UGH! FINE!
YOU WANT ME TO LEAVE THEN, IS THAT RIGHT!?
PLEASE BE CAREFUL.
I'LL FINISH AND COME BACK RIGHT AWAY!

YOU TWO SEEM CLOSE.
IT SEEMS SHE'S TAKEN A LIKING TO ME FOR SOME REASON.
SASHA-SAN ONLY CAME TO THIS TOWN RECENTLY, RIGHT?
YES.
OH!
M-MAYBE SHE'S...
...A STALKER?
YOU'RE OVER-THINKING IT.
NO, I'M NOT!
YOU NEVER CAN BE SURE! IF ANYTHING HAPPENS, TELL ME!
NGHH...
BUT YOU DID COME GALLANTLY DASHING IN TO SAVE HER...
NGHHHHH?
NGHH? NGHH?
AGH!
I KNOW EXACTLY HOW THAT FEELS! UGH!
...

I THOUGHT THAT IF SHE HAD SURVIVED, SHE WOULD HAVE ENDED UP A SLAVE.
HAAAAH!
IT'S SO NICE TO HAVE A PERFECTLY ORDINARY DAY!
WHEN IT'S NORMAL, IT'S THE BEST! ♪
...!

OH... HEE-HEE. WAS THAT A LITTLE DRAMAT-IC?
...NO.
I DON'T LIKE HOW BUSY WE WERE, LIKE HOW IT WAS EARLIER.
I GET FLUSTERED RIGHT AWAY AND START MAKING MISTAKES.
OH, RIGHT! DID YOU HEAR THAT I'M COMING OVER AFTER WORK?
YES, IN ORDER TO TEACH RILA HOW TO COOK, WAS IT?
YES! I HOPE YOU'RE LOOKING FORWARD TO IT!
LET'S KEEP IT UP FOR THE LAST STRETCH OF THE WORKDAY!
HURRAH!
PLEASE APPRAISE THESE.
HEY.
WHEN IT'S ***NORMAL,*** *IT'S THE BEST...*
WHAT A VERY WISE THING TO SAY.

IS THERE SOMETHING HAPPENING OUTSIDE?
SASHA-SAN SAID SHE'D COME BACK TODAY.
OH, BUT IT'S PRETTY COMMON FOR PEOPLE TO REPORT THE NEXT DAY.
IT WAS A GATH-ERING QUEST.
I SEE...THAT DOES SEEM UNUSUAL.
ESPECIALLY SINCE IT'S COMMON FOR OTHERS TO STEAL THE HERBS.
I WONDER IF SOMETHING HAPPENED TO HER...
THE WOODS AREN'T FAR, SO I'LL CHECK ON HER.
I'M SORRY. PLEASE TELL RILA FOR ME.
HUH!? ROLAND-SAN!?
TA (TMP)

A D-RANK ADVENTURER, HUH...
KNOCKED HER OUT FROM BEHIND WITH ONE BLOW, THOUGH.
NOT MUCH OF ONE, I'D SAY.

SO, WHAT'LL WE DO WITH THIS GIRLIE?
HER FACE AIN'T TOO BAD.
WE CAN SELL HER OFF TO A SLAVER AFTER HAVING SOME FUN WITH HER.
POOR THING.
BET SHE'S BEEN TAKEN ADVANTAGE OF PLENTY BY MEN AFTER BECOMING AN ADVENTURER.
TWO MORE GUYS SHOULD BE NO PROBLEM FOR HER.
PACHI (CRACKLE)
PACHI
SHE MIGHT WAKE UP.
THINK SHE'LL STRUGGLE?
THAT JUST MAKES IT BETTER IN A WAY.

GAAAAAAAH!?
JU (SZZ)
BASA (FLAP)
SA
SA
NOW THAT'S A SUREFIRE WAY TO CAUSE ME TROUBLE.
YEEEK! WHAT THE—!? WHAT IN THE—!?
GET LOST, SCUM.
HUH!? WHO THE HELL ARE YOU!?
TARRY TOO LONG AND I'LL CHOP OFF CERTAIN BODY PARTS...
...TO USE IN PLACE OF KINDLING.
MY SWORD!
THAT'S NOT FAIR!

OR WOULD YOU RATHER ...
KA (THUNK)
AGH!
SU (SWIP)
...THAT I STICK IT ALL THE WAY IN THIS TIME?
PACHI
PACHI (CRACKLE)
PACHI
YIKES...
HM...

HUH?
WHAT AM I—?
YOU HIT YOUR HEAD AND FAINTED IN THE WOODS.
ARGAN-SAN, WHY ARE YOU...?
I SEE...
I'LL TAKE YOU TO YOUR INN.
JUST A GUILD STAFFER'S INTUITION.
SO THAT MAKES THIS THE THIRD TIME.
IT'S THE SECOND.

IF ANYTHING FEELS OFF, GO TO THE DOCTOR RIGHT AWAY.
OKAY.
IF YOU'LL EXCUSE ME.
COULD I...
OH!
GU (TUG)
UM...
C-COULD I THANK YOU THIS EVENING?

PAN (SLAP)
I BELIEVE YOU'VE MIS-UNDERSTOOD SOMETHING.

YOU WERE QUICKER THAN I ANTICI-PATED.
YES...
MILIA SAID YOU WOULD BE LATE.
YES...
YOU DARE GIVE ME THOSE HALF-HEARTED REPLIES!?
WHAT AILS YOU? YOU HAVE BEEN PENSIVE THE LAST FEW DAYS. IS SOMETHING BOTHERING YOU?
HA HA HA...
IS IRIS PICKING ON YOU?
WELL, IF YOU MUST TALK ABOUT IT...
...I SUPPOSE I MIGHT LEND YOU AN EAR.
COME NOW.
UKI
UKI (EAGER)
WAKU (GLEE)
WAKU
...
HAAH...
IT'S NOT A FUN STORY...
I DO NOT MIND! NOW, TELL ME.

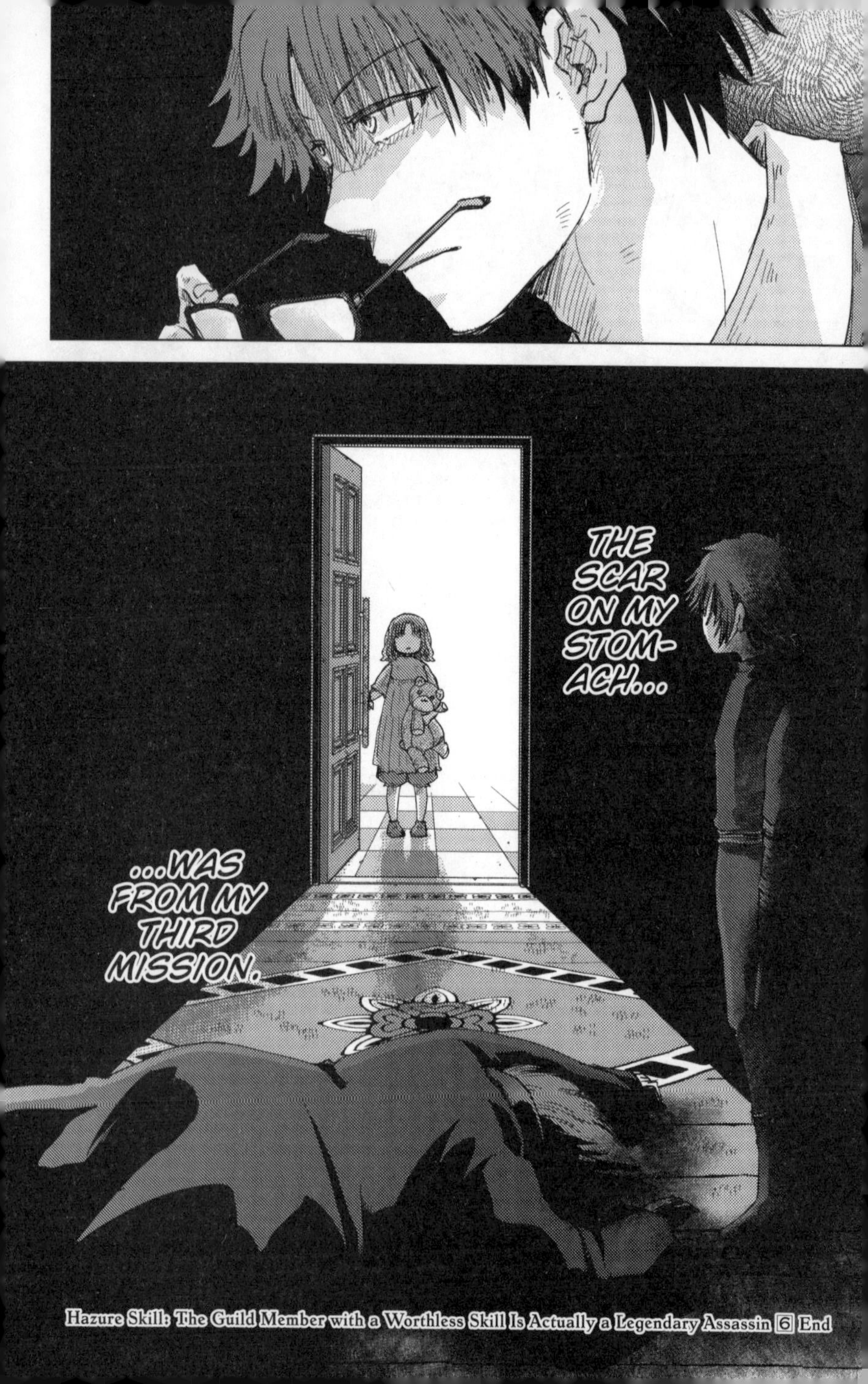

Hazure Skill: The Guild Member with a Worthless Skill Is Actually a Legendary Assassin 6 End

WE'RE AT THE SIXTH VOLUME! I ENDED UP GETTING SICK, SO I'M SORRY FOR THE DELAY! BY THE TIME THIS BOOK IS ON SALE, I SHOULD HAVE CUT OUT ANYTHING UNNECESSARY IN MY LIFE AND MADE A FULL RECOVERY, SO I CAN GET THE SEVENTH VOLUME TO YOU RIGHT AWAY!! ...IN MY DREAMS. I'LL WORK AS FAST AS I CAN SO WE CAN MEET AGAIN SOON. I HOPE TO SEE YOU IN THE NEXT ONE.

FUH ARAKI

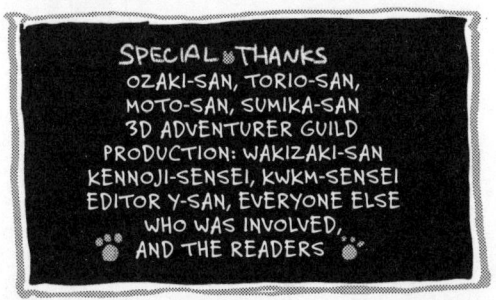

THERE WERE LOTS OF BACKGROUND CHARACTERS I LIKED IN THIS ONE. ☺

SPECIAL THANKS
OZAKI-SAN, TORIO-SAN,
MOTO-SAN, SUMIKA-SAN
3D ADVENTURER GUILD
PRODUCTION: WAKIZAKI-SAN
KENNOJI-SENSEI, KWKM-SENSEI
EDITOR Y-SAN, EVERYONE ELSE
WHO WAS INVOLVED,
AND THE READERS

THE NOBLE DEMON LORD, KITTY RILA

FUH ARAKI

CAT EDITION

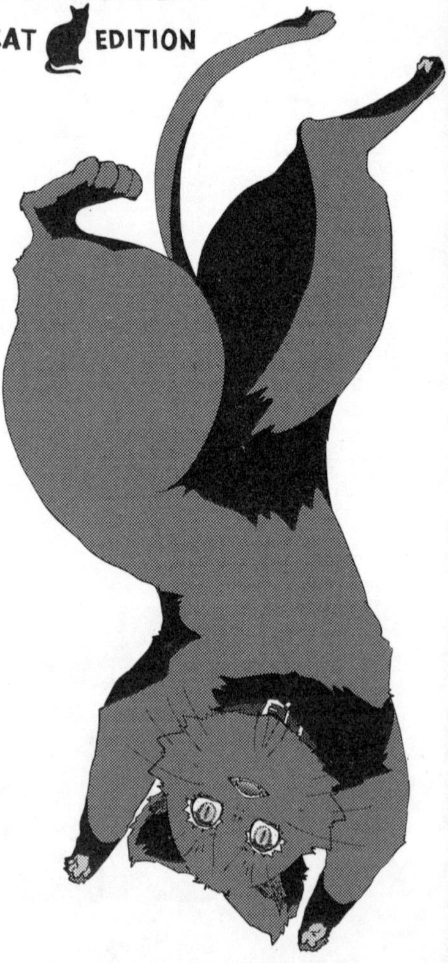

OH, ROLAND-SAAAN!
SHAKE.
BESHI (PLIT)
IT MUST BE BECAUSE YOU'RE HER OWNER!
I COULDN'T EMBARRASS MY PARTNER!
WE NORMALLY DON'T DO THIS.
OH, IT'S THE BOSS CAT! IT'S BEEN FOREVER!
SHAKE!
WOW, SO YOU CAN DO IT!
PECHIN (SLAP)
BISHI! (PLAP)
OH WOW!
OF COURSE I AM CAPABLE OF ANYTHING ANOTHER CAT CAN DO!
HEH HEH!

DON'T YOU THINK YOU'VE WORKED OUT ENOUGH ALREADYYY !?!?
HFF!
HFF!
HFF!
HEY!!
THERE'S NO SUCH THING AS TOO MUCH PREPARATION!
THE HERO IS OVERPOWERED BUT OVERLY CAUTIOUS
AVAILABLE NOW!
YEN ON
Yen Press
For more information visit www.yenpress.com
KONO YUSHA GA ORE TUEEE KUSENI SHINCHO SUGIRU
©Koyuki 2019 ©Light Tuchihi, Saori Toyota 2019 / KADOKAWA CORPORATION
KONO YUSHA GA ORE TUEEE KUSENI SHINCHO SUGIRU
©Light Tuchihi, Saori Toyota 2017 / KADOKAWA CORPORATION
LIGHT NOVEL
MANGA

COMBATANTS WILL BE DISPATCHED!
LIGHT NOVEL
VOLUMES 1-6
MANGA
VOLUMES 1-7
AVAILABLE NOW WHEREVER BOOKS ARE SOLD!
With world domination nearly in their grasp, the Supreme Leaders of the Kisaragi Corporation—an underground criminal group turned evil megacorp—have decided to try their hands at interstellar conquest. A quick dice roll nominates their chief operative, Combat Agent Six, to be the one to explore an alien planet...and the first thing he does when he gets there is change the sacred incantation for a holy ritual to the most embarrassing thing he can think of. But evil deeds are business as usual for Kisaragi operatives, so if Six wants a promotion and a raise, he'll have to work much harder than that! For starters, he'll have to do something about the other group of villains on the planet, who are calling themselves the "Demon Lord's Army" or whatever. After all, this world doesn't need two evil organizations!
YEN ON
Yen Press
For more information visit www.yenpress.com
©Masaaki Kiasa 2018©Natsume Akatsuki, Kakao • Lanthanum 2018 / KADOKAWA CORPORATION
©Natsume Akatsuki, Kakao • Lanthanum 2017 / KADOKAWA CORPORATION

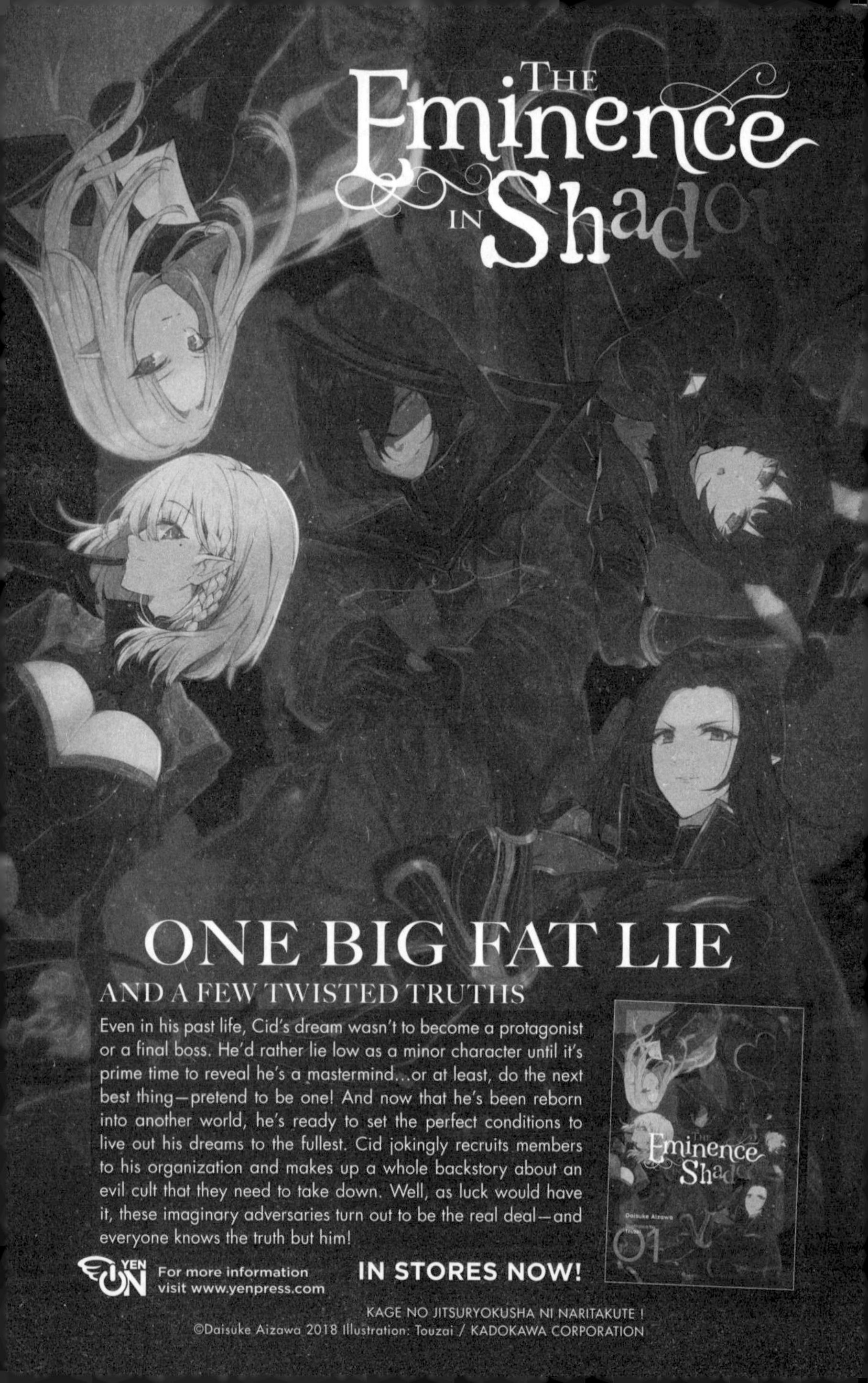
THE Eminence IN Shadow
ONE BIG FAT LIE
AND A FEW TWISTED TRUTHS
Even in his past life, Cid's dream wasn't to become a protagonist or a final boss. He'd rather lie low as a minor character until it's prime time to reveal he's a mastermind…or at least, do the next best thing—pretend to be one! And now that he's been reborn into another world, he's ready to set the perfect conditions to live out his dreams to the fullest. Cid jokingly recruits members to his organization and makes up a whole backstory about an evil cult that they need to take down. Well, as luck would have it, these imaginary adversaries turn out to be the real deal—and everyone knows the truth but him!
The Eminence in Shadow
Daisuke Aizawa
01
YEN ON
For more information visit www.yenpress.com
IN STORES NOW!
KAGE NO JITSURYOKUSHA NI NARITAKUTE !
©Daisuke Aizawa 2018 Illustration: Touzai / KADOKAWA CORPORATION

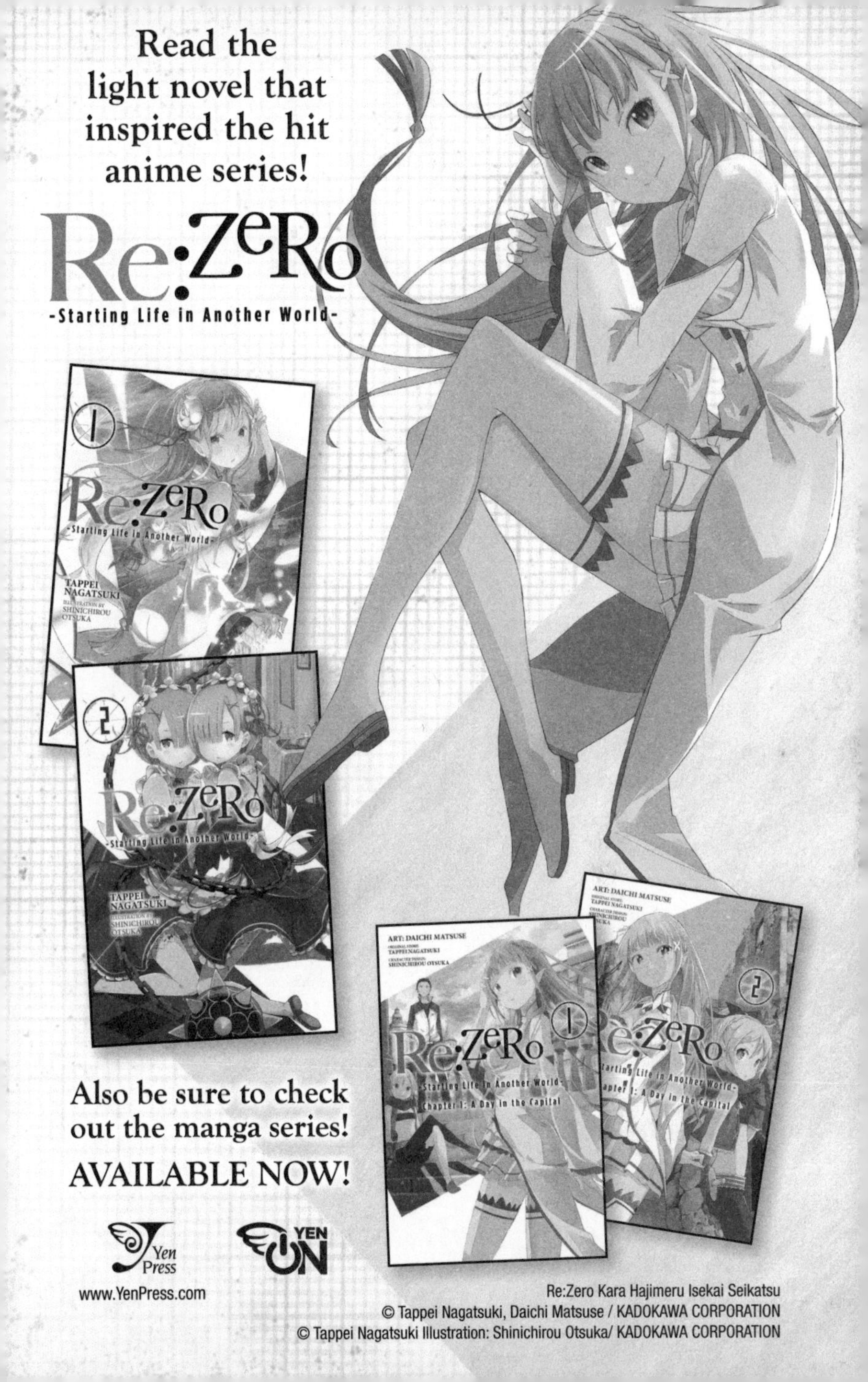

Read the light novel that inspired the hit anime series!
Re:ZeRo
-Starting Life in Another World-
Also be sure to check out the manga series!
AVAILABLE NOW!
Yen Press
YEN ON
www.YenPress.com
Re:Zero Kara Hajimeru Isekai Seikatsu
© Tappei Nagatsuki, Daichi Matsuse / KADOKAWA CORPORATION
© Tappei Nagatsuki Illustration: Shinichirou Otsuka/ KADOKAWA CORPORATION

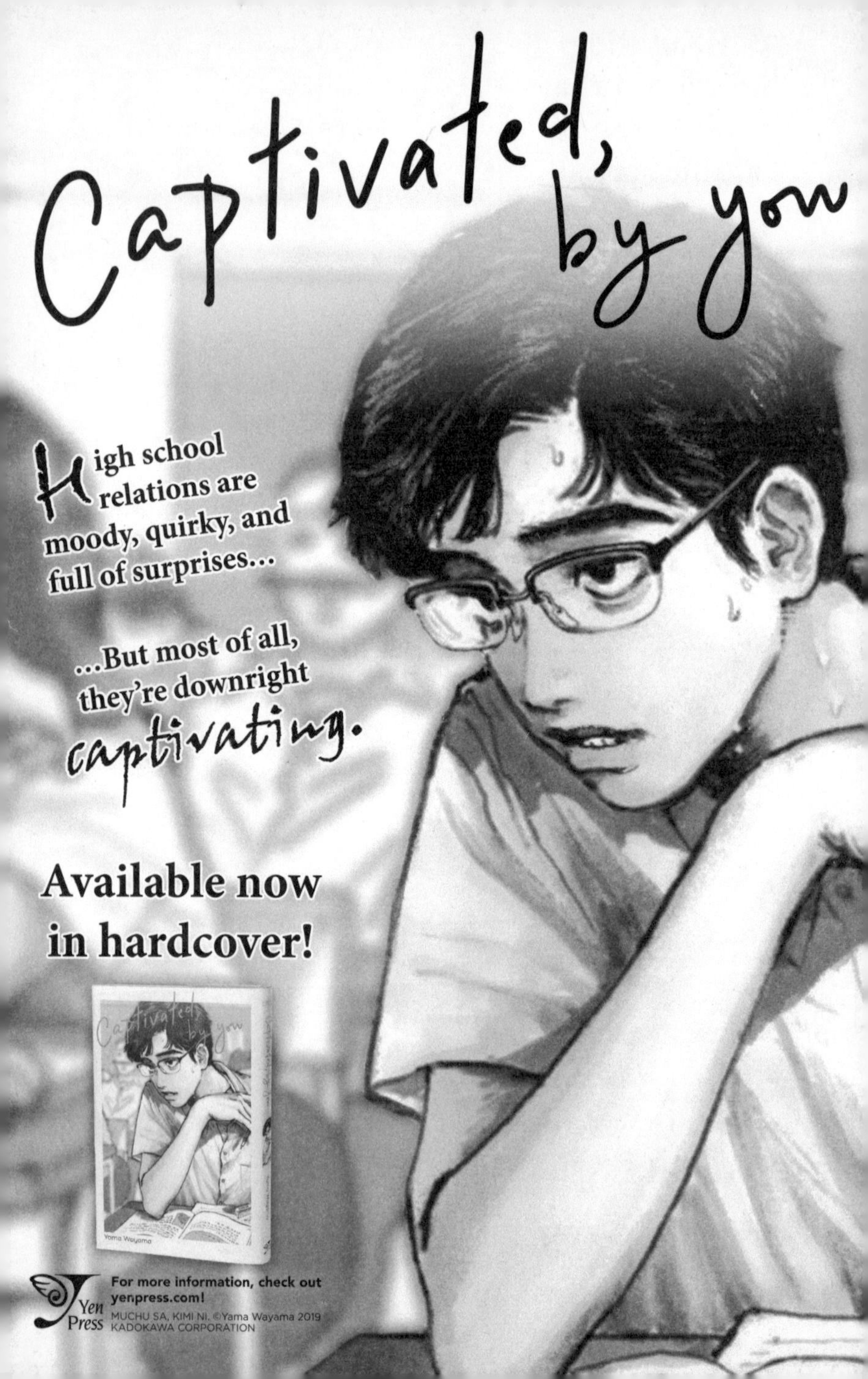
Captivated, by you
High school relations are moody, quirky, and full of surprises...
...But most of all, they're downright captivating.
Available now in hardcover!
Captivated, by you
Yama Wayama
Yen Press
For more information, check out yenpress.com!
MUCHU SA, KIMI NI. ©Yama Wayama 2019 KADOKAWA CORPORATION

From the New York Times bestselling author of Durarara!! comes
a light novel series full of mobsters, thieves, and immortals!
BACCANO!
VOLUMES 1–21 AVAILABLE NOW
BACCANO!
The Rolling Bootlegs
RYOHGO NARITA
BACCANO!
RYOHGO NARITA
BACCANO!
RYOHGO NARITA
BACCANO!
RYOHGO NARITA
2017
YEN ON
USA
WWW.YENPRESS.COM
"BACCANO! © RYOHGO NARITA ILLUSTRATION: KATSUMI ENAMI
KADOKAWA CORPORATION ASCII MEDIA WORKS"

HAZURE SKILL 6

THE GUILD MEMBER WITH A WORTHLESS SKILL IS ACTUALLY A LEGENDARY ASSASSIN

Fuh Araki ORIGINAL STORY Kennoji CHARACTER DESIGN KWKM

TRANSLATION Jan Mitsuko Cash LETTERING Carolina Hdz

Yen Press
150 West 30th Street, 19th Floor
New York, NY 10001

Visit us at yenpress.com † facebook.com/yenpress † twitter.com/yenpress † yenpress.tumblr.com † instagram.com/yenpress

First Yen Press Edition: March 2024
Edited by Yen Press Editorial: Mark Gallucci
Designed by Yen Press Design: Jane Sohn, Andy Swist

Yen Press is an imprint of Yen Press, LLC.
The Yen Press name and logo are trademarks of Yen Press, LLC.

The publisher is not responsible for websites (or their content) that are not owned by the publisher.

Library of Congress Control Number: 2021930391

ISBNs: 978-1-9753-8047-2 (paperback)
978-1-9753-8048-9 (ebook)

1 3 5 7 9 10 8 6 4 2

WOR

Printed in the United States of America

IS IT WRONG TO TRY TO PICK UP GIRLS IN A DUNGEON? ON THE SIDE: SWORD ORATORIA ③

Fujino Omori
Takashi Yagi
Haimura Kiyotaka, Yasuda Suzuhito

Translation: Andrew Gaippe • Lettering: Brndn Blakeslee

Yen Press
1290 Avenue of the Americas
New York, NY 10104

Visit us at yenpress.com
facebook.com/yenpress
twitter.com/yenpress
yenpress.tumblr.com
instagram.com/yenpress

First Yen Press Edition: April 2018

Yen Press is an imprint of Yen Press, LLC.
The Yen Press name and logo are trademarks of Yen Press, LLC.

The publisher is not responsible for websites (or their content) that are not owned by the publisher.

Library of Congress Control Number: 2016946068

ISBNs: 978-0-316-44796-6 (paperback)
978-0-316-44798-0 (ebook)

10 9 8 7 6 5 4 3 2 1

WOR

Printed in the United States of America

Is it WRONG to TRY to PiCK UP GIRLS iN A DUNGEON? ON THE SiDE
SWORD ORATORIA
TAKASHI YAGI
ORIGINAL STORY FUJINO OMORI
CHARACTER DESIGN KIYOTAKA HAIMURA
SUZUHITO YASUDA

3

SWORD ORATORIA

CONTENTS

quest 9. Next Quest

WEIGHT.
HYU (FWOOSH)
KYU (WHOOSH)
BAL-ANCE.
KI (SHING)
GRIP.
PA
CUT-TING EDGE.
PA
PA
PA (SWING)
ADJUST-MENTS COMPLETE.
BI (SHING)

BI
(SLASH)
BI
BI
BI
PI
(CRACK)
ZAAA
(FLUTTER)
CHAKI
(CLINK)
LEFIYA
...!
TH...THAT
WAS AMAZING,
AIZ-SAN!
S-SORRY,
IT WAS SO
CAPTIVAT-
ING......
...THAT I
FORGOT TO
ANNOUNCE
MYSELF...
UM...
THANK
YOU?

SO, IT IS TRUE YOU PRACTICE THIS EARLY IN THE MORNING.
THAT'S WHY YOU'RE SO STRONG...
I MUST LEARN FROM YOUR EXAMPLE!!
WHO INSTRUCTED YOU IN THE ART OF SWORDS-MANSHIP?
...MY FATHER, I GUESS...
IS THAT SO!?
EVEN AS A MAGIC USER, I CAN TELL YOU'VE REALLY HONED YOUR TECHNIQUE...
SO, IT'S FROM YOUR FATHER...

IF I MAY ASK, WHAT ARE YOUR PARENTS DOING NOW...?
LEFIYA, HOW MUCH TIME DOES IT TAKE TO RETRIEVE ONE BOOK?
R-RIVERIA-SAMA ...!!
YOU HAVE YOUR OWN TRAINING TO ATTEND.
AND YOU, AIZ? IT HAS BEEN A WHILE SINCE YOU LAST JOINED US.
PAA (GLOW)
PHYSICAL STRENGTH IS NOT ALL THAT'S REQUIRED TO IMPROVE.
I SEE. THAT IS UNFORTUNATE. LEFIYA.
WE SHALL CONTINUE UNTIL BREAKFAST.
A...AIZ-SAAAN!

JYAN (TA-DAA)
MY HAIR, PERFECT!
APRON, PERFECT!!
HOME-COOKED BREAKFAST, PERFECT!!!
YOU THERE!
HE DOESN'T NEED ANY DISHES!!
THE CAPTAIN'S BREAKFAST IS RIGHT HERE!!
Sir...
I have some particularly good meds for indigestion, if you'd like some...
HA-HA... THAT'D BE GREAT.

!!
GIKU (FLINCH)
OH ...
BETE-SAN... GOOD MORNING.
...H-HEY.
GIKU
SHAKU (TWITCH)
GIKU
SHAKU
?
GOOD MORN-ING, AIZ!
GABA (POUNCE)
MORNING, TIONA.
LET'S CHOW DOWN!
JUST IGNORE THE SHAMEFUL WOLFY WHO CAN'T HOLD HIS ALCOHOL OR LOOK YOU IN THE EYE.
GAH!!
UM ...!

KURU (GLANCE)
BE (PULL)
!!
GET OFF YOUR HIGH HORSE, YOU STICK WOMAN!!
HUH !!?
YOU BETTER TAKE THAT BACK RIGHT NOOOOOOOW!!
SUCH A RUCKUS AT THE CRACK O' DAWN!!
KEEP IT QUIET IN THE HALLS, WOULD YA!!
URRRRR
THE THREE OF YA, TAKE A SEAT!
TOP-CLASS ADVENTURERS GOTTA ACT THE PART! I'LL WHIP YA INTA SHAPE RIGHT NOW!!
WHAT. ME TOO ...!?
KUDO (RANT)
KUDO
GESHI (SMACK)
GESHI
PASHA (WHACK)
PASHA

OWW... MY LEGS HURT...
ARE YOU ALL RIGHT?
I SET ASIDE ENOUGH FOOD FOR BOTH OF YOU.
THANK YOU, LEFIYA.
THIS MORNING'S MEAL IS FULL OF DEMETER FAMILIA'S FRESH VEGETABLES.
ALSO, TO HELP YOU RECOVER FROM YOUR MORNING TRAINING SESSION, AIZ-SAN...
...I'VE PREPARED LEMON-HONEY TEA.
SINCE YOU ARE STRANGELY ACTIVE THIS MORNING, TIONA-SAN...
...I'VE MADE YOU A CUP OF HERBAL TEA TO HELP YOU RELAX.
AND I'M DRINKING THE SAME TEA AS YOU, AIZ-SAN! ♡
....
SAY, AIZ, WHA'CHA DOING TODAY?
AH... YES.
ACTUALLY, YESTERDAY AT GOIBNIU FAMILIA...
IN THIS CONDITION AFTER ONLY FIVE DAYS......

DAAAMN THAT AMAZON! BURN IN HEEEELL!!
KAAN (CLANG)
KAAN
YOU YOUNG 'UNS SURE KNOW HOW TO MAKE A BLACK-SMITH CRY.
KAAN
KAAN
KAAN
... Sorry.
...... HOW MUCH WILL IT COST?
FORTY MILLION VALIS...
...OR THERE-ABOUTS.
V40,000,000
GON (THUD)
I'LL HAVE TO PROWL THE DUNGEON FOR A WEEK TO MAKE THAT MUCH...
GATA (SHAKE)
GATA
IS THAT ALL? I'LL JOIN YOU!!
HUH? BUT...
M-ME TOO! IF IT'S NOT A BOTHER!
I'VE GOT TO PAY OFF URGA TOO, YOU KNOW!
...

WE'LL BE GONE FOR A WHILE, SO DON'CHA THINK WE SHOULD TELL FINN?
THE NEXT EXPEDITION IS STILL WELL OFF, BUT...
...I AGREE.
TIONE—!
THE THREE OF US ARE HITTING THE DUNGEON FOR A WEEK. WANNA COME?
...OKAY. THEN PLEASE JOIN ME.
HUH? WASN'T THAT FOR FINN?
YEAH.

THE CAPTAIN SAID IT WOULD BE A WASTE FOR HIM TO EAT ALL THIS ON HIS OWN...
...SO HE LET ME HAVE HALF. ♡
PAKU (MUNCH)
HEE-HEE... SO THIS IS WHAT IT'S LIKE TO SHARE A MEAL.
HEE-HEE-HEE... ♡
HALF ...?
THAT'S ALMOST ALL OF IT, ISN'T IT...?
WELL, TIONE ...?
I'LL PASS. A WEEK WITHOUT SEEING THE CAPTAIN IS FAR TOO LONG.
WE WERE GONNA INVITE HIM TOO.
PIKU (TWITCH)
GA (CHOMP)
GUI (LIFT)
GA
GA
KARAN (CLATTER)
BON (THUNK)
KYU (SQUEAK)

THEN I GUESS I HAVE NO CHOICE.
I'LL COME ALONG!
BE GRATE-FUL.
YAAAAY!
FINN— YOU IN HERE?
GACHA (CLICK)

WHAT'S GOTTEN INTO ALL OF YOU, BARGING IN LIKE THAT?
AH... RIVERIA-SAMA, PLEASE EXCUSE US...
HMM... PLEASE GIVE US A MOMENT. WE'RE ALMOST FINISHED.
THAT... SHOULD DO IT.
SO, WHAT'S ON YOUR MIND?
YOU SEE, MY SISTER AND THESE TWO HERE ARE GOING TO SPEND SOME TIME IN THE DUNGEON...
...AND WANTED TO ASK YOU TO JOIN THEM, CAPTAIN...
OH, SURE.
YES!
I WAS THINKING ABOUT TAKING A JAUNT INTO THE DUNGEON SOON, ANYWAY.
IT'S NICE TO PROWL AT YOUR OWN PACE EVERY NOW AND THEN.

CARE TO JOIN US, RIVERIA?
...YES, I BELIEVE I WOULD.
I GUESS GARETH... WILL HAVE TO TAKE CHARGE DURING OUR ABSENCE.
OH!
DON'T MENTION THIS TO BETE! THERE'LL BE NO KEEPING HIM BACK IF HE FINDS OUT! AND HE'S SO ANNOYING!!
WEEELL... IT WOULDN'T BE GOOD TO HAVE ALL OF OUR STRONGEST MEMBERS LEAVE THE MANOR AT ONCE.
THEN IT'S SETTLED. MAKE YOUR OWN PREPARATIONS AND MEET UP AT BABEL TOWER AT NOON?
YEAH—!!

DIAN CECHT FAMILIA'S TREATMENT CENTER
WEL-COME.
AMID! GIMME THE BEST HIGH POTIONS YOU GOT!
THE GOOD STUFF, AND LOTS OF 'EM!
I'D LIKE FIVE OF THE SAME... PLEASE. A MIND POTION TOO.
PLUS THESE ITEMS ON THIS LIST...
UNDER-STOOD.
KATA (TMP)
カタッ
PURU (WOBBLE)
PURU
プルプル
...NEED A HAND?
THANK YOU FOR YOUR CONCERN, BUT I KNOW WHAT I'M DOING.
PURU
PURU
PURU
PURU
DON'T LOOK AT ME LIKE THAT. I MAY NOT LOOK LIKE IT...
...BUT I'M OLDER THAN BOTH OF YOU.
PLEASE DO NOT PAT MY HEAD.
NADE (PAT)
NADE
なで
なで

AMID, SINCE WE'RE HEADING INTO THE DUNGEON, NEED ANYTHING WHILE WE'RE THERE?
WE'LL GET DOWN TO THE THIRTIETH FLOOR AT LEAST.
IN THAT CASE... MAY I ASK YOU TO RETRIEVE SEVERAL WHITE LEAVES?
CONSIDER IT DOOONE! ♪
I AWAIT YOUR NEXT VISIT.
PLEASE STAY SAFE.
MAGIC-USER SUPPLY SHOP "WITCH'S HIDEAWAY"
GII (CREAK)
LENOA, WE ARE COMING INSIDE.
AHH, RIVERIA, SO YOU'VE COME... WHAT'S THIS? BROUGHT THE GIRL TODAY?
I-IT HAS BEEN A LONG TIME.
HAVE THE MAGIC CRYSTALS BEEN RE-PLACED?

INDEED, THEY HAVE.
WITH THE SPECIAL ONES, JUST AS YOU ASKED.
I HAVE NO IDEA WHAT YOU DO ON THOSE EXPEDITIONS, BUT BREAKING FOUR CRYSTALS AT ONCE IS UNHEARD OF......
A MAGIC USER'S STAFF INCREASES NOT ONLY THE WIELDER'S MAGIC POWER BUT THEIR MAGIC'S INTENSITY AS WELL.
MAGIC CRYSTALS ARE THE CONDUIT.
MAGES LIKE MYSELF ARE THE ONLY ONES WHO CAN MAKE THEM. THEY'RE QUITE VALUABLE.
I AM WELL AWARE. THEY ARE NOT BEING WASTED.
EH!?
ISN'T... ISN'T THAT A GRIMOIRE!?
YOU DON'T EXPECT ME TO BELIEVE YOU CREATED IT, LENOA?
EE-HEE-HEE! I'M NOT THAT POWERFUL OF A MAGE.
I HAVE AN ACQUAINTANCE IN ALTINA...
...WHO WAS GRACIOUS ENOUGH TO SHARE.

GOT SEVERAL REGULARS BIDDING ON THIS ONE. HEE-HEE... GETTING UP THERE, DON'T YOU THINK?
¥130.400.000
I-IT'S... ASTRONOMICAL.
OF COURSE.
ONE LEARNS MAGIC BY SIMPLY READING IT. IT IS A BOOK THAT FORCES MAGIC ACQUISITION.
SHOULD ITS ORIGIN TRULY BE THE MAGIC KINGDOM OF ALTINA, THERE'S A CHANCE IT WILL SIMULTANEOUSLY GRANT AN EXTRA MAGIC SLOT IN THE READER'S STATUS AS WELL.
THAT'S ASSUMING THEY HAVE LESS THAN THREE MAGIC SPELLS ALREADY...
...BUT IT'S USELESS FOR OUTLIERS SUCH AS YOURSELVES **WHO CAN CAST MORE THAN FOUR.**
MANY IN ALTINA HAVE THEIR EYES ON YOU TWO.
M-ME TOO!?
COME, YOUNG GIRL, HAVE YOU FORGOTTEN YOU POSSESS THE FLASHY TITLE "THOUSAND ELF"?
EE-HEE-HEE! WATCH YOUR BACK AT NIGHT.

ENOUGH WITH MEANINGLESS THREATS, LENOA.
LEFIYA, DO NOT TAKE HER SERIOUSLY.
Y-YES!
YOU'RE NO FUN, RIVERIA.
...HEE-HEE. COME AGAIN.
BATAN (CLOSE)
GUILD HEADQUARTERS LOBBY
IT'S NICE TO TAKE A NORMAL QUEST EVERY NOW AND THEN.
YES.
AIZ AND TIONA NEED TO PAY OFF THEIR WEAPON DEBTS...
WE'RE GOING ANYWAY, SO WHY NOT HAVE A LOOK?
WE NEED MONEY, RIGHT?
Especially that idiot sister of mine who ordered an adamantite weapon without a second thought...
She took out a loan like you wouldn't believe.
I'LL PAY YOU BACK NEXT TIME!
WE WON'T LET YOU IN THE DOOR AGAIN UNTIL YOU DO!
BETTER YET, DON'T BOTHER COMING BACK!!

SO, WE NEED A LOT OF SIMPLE ONES WITH HIGH REWARDS...
SOUNDS LIKE MONSTER-TYPE QUESTS WOULD BE OUR BEST BET.
OH? THIS LOOKS INTERESTING.
WHAT'S THAT?
"SONG ECHOING THROUGH THE DUNGEON" ...PLEASE FIND THE SOURCE OF THE SONG I HEARD IN THE DEEP LEVELS.
I CAN'T TELL IF THE SINGER IS HUMAN, MONSTER, OR THE DUNGEON ITSELF...
THE CLIENT IS SO INTRIGUED HE CAN'T SLEEP AT NIGHT.
WOW... IT'S NOT A MONSTER'S HOWL, BUT CAPTIVATING ENOUGH TO MAKE THIS GUY FALL IN LOVE.
THAT'S NO GOOD, CAPTAIN.
IT'S NOTHING MORE THAN A WILD-GOOSE CHASE.
THE REWARD IS NEXT TO NOTHING.
WE DON'T HAVE TIME FOR THIS SORT OF THING.
NOW, WHERE'S YOUR SENSE OF ADVENTURE?

DUNGEON ENTRANCE
BABEL TOWER
CENTRAL PARK
AH! THAT'S FINN AND TIONE.
WE'RE THE LAST ONES HERE?
SORRY TO KEEP YOU WAITING. LET'S GO.
HAAH...IT HAS BEEN A WHILE SINCE WE HAVE GONE INTO THE DUNGEON LIKE THIS.
HEE-HEE! I'VE BEEN SO EXCITED ALL MORNING...!
I GUESS WE SHOULD TRY TO HOLD BACK A LITTLE...
AIZ-SAN...
I...UM...THANK YOU FOR BRINGING ME ALONG FOR THIS JOURNEY!
I'M...SO HAPPY!
...I...

...IT WAS CARELESS OF ME TO BREAK MY SWORD...
SO, IS IT OKAY TO DRAG EVERYONE TO THE DUNGEON BECAUSE OF ME...?
I THOUGHT I SHOULD REFUSE.
BUT RIGHT NOW...
...HERE WITH EVERY-ONE...
...I THINK I'M HAPPY TO HAVE COMPANY.

I WILL DO EVERYTHING I CAN TO BE USEFUL!!
YES, THANK YOU, LEFIYA.
LET'S TRY OUR BEST.
AIZ, LEFIYA!
COME ON!

DO (THUMP)
DO
DO
DO
HEEEYAAAAA
AAAAHHHH!!
DO
KI (SLASH)
ALL RIGHT!! URGA'S BACK AND BETTER THAN EVER!!
WATCH IT...
YOU'LL POKE SOME-ONE'S EYE OUT.
JUST AN EYE?
PASHI (SWING)

PAY ATTENTION, LEFIYA!!
FACE FORWARD!!
YE—
EEEEK!?
GOO (ROAR)
HIYA—!
GA (WHACK)
HIT THE THROAT!!
ZU (STAB)
YES!!
I BELIEVE YOU ARE TOO ACCUSTOMED TO FIGHTING FROM A DISTANCE WITH MAGIC.
YOU HAVE A HABIT OF PANICKING WHEN AN ENEMY IS CLOSE BY. CALM YOUR MIND.
CLOSE-QUARTERS COMBAT IS VITAL, EVEN FOR MAGIC USERS. REMEMBER THAT.
Y-YES, MA'AM!!
ZUZUN (SHUDDER)

FLOOR SEVENTEEN ALREADY.
SHOULDN'T BE SURPRISED WITH A PARTY LIKE THIS, THOUGH.
CONSIDERING HOW MUCH WE NEED TO MAKE...
...COLLECTING MAGIC STONES IN THE UPPER LEVELS ISN'T WORTH OUR TIME.
OKAY!
CUT DOWN THE MONSTERS THAT ATTACK, AND IGNORE EVERYTHING ELSE!
GAKU (TREMBLE) GAKU
FULL SPEED AHEAD!
YEAH!!
BURU (SHAKE) BURU
GENERALLY, THE LOWER THE FLOOR, THE STRONGER THE MONSTERS.
THEREFORE, MAGIC STONES INCREASE IN QUALITY...
...AND DROP ITEMS GROW IN RARITY AND PRICE DEEPER IN THE DUNGEON.
RATHER THAN STAYING IN THE MIDDLE LEVELS, THERE'S A FAR BETTER CHANCE OF ACQUIRING MORE-VALUABLE LOOT IN THE LOWER AND DEEP LEVELS.

HOWEVER, ADVENTURERS MUST FIRST PASS THROUGH TWO AREAS TO REACH THOSE FLOORS.
THE FIRST IS A MASSIVE CHAMBER WHERE GOLIATH APPEARS.
THE FLOOR BOSS, GOLIATH, IS COMPLETELY DIFFERENT FROM THE AVERAGE MONSTER— A MONSTER REX.
EVEN UPPER-CLASS ADVENTURERS MUST FORM LARGE PARTIES TO TAKE DOWN THIS MONSTROSITY.
HOWEVER, UNLIKE NORMAL DUNGEON MONSTERS THAT ARE ALWAYS BEING BORN, GOLIATH, ONCE DEFEATED, TAKES TWO WEEKS TO RESPAWN.
THE SECOND AREA IS ONLY ACCESSIBLE DURING THOSE TWO WEEKS AND TO THE PARTY OF ADVENTURERS WHO MANAGED TO OVERCOME ITS PROTECTOR...
...FOR BEYOND GOLIATH...
WHAT?
THE GOLIATH'S NOT HERE. DID SOMEONE TAKE IT DOWN?
TA (STEP) TA TA
YES. I'M PRETTY SURE RIVIRA'S ADVENTURERS TOOK CARE OF IT.
IT GETS IN THE WAY.

...IS FLOOR EIGHTEEN'S "UNDER RESORT"

IT'S THE FIRST "SAFE POINT" ADVENTURERS VISIT ON THEIR TRAVELS.
"A FLOOR WHERE MONSTERS ARE NOT BORN."
YEEES! FINALLY, BREAK TIMEEE!
THIS PLACE IS ALWAYS BEAUTIFUL NO MATTER WHEN I COME.
IT APPEARS TO BE "DAY" RIGHT NOW.
DESPITE BEING DEEP UNDERGROUND, THIS FLOOR HAS A "SKY."
A MASSIVE CRYSTAL FORMATION COVERS THE CEILING.
A LARGE WHITE CRYSTAL IN ITS CENTER PRODUCES VARYING AMOUNTS OF LIGHT...
...WHICH CREATES A "MORNING," "DAY," AND "NIGHT" CYCLE DIFFERENT FROM THE SURFACE.

THE FLOOR'S OTHER DEFINING CHARAC-TERISTIC...
...IS AS A REST STOP TOWN CALLED "RIVIRA" RUN COMPLETELY BY UPPER-CLASS ADVENTURERS.
IT FEELS LIKE AGES SINCE I'VE BEEN HERE.
334
FELLOW ADVENTURERS WELCOME TO RIVIRA
UM...I HAVE BEEN CURIOUS ABOUT THIS FOR A WHILE, BUT...THAT NUMBER ON THE SIGN, COULD IT MEAN...
OH, THAT? IT MEANS THIS IS THE 334TH RIVIRA.
IN OTHER WORDS, IT'S BEEN WIPED OUT 333 TIMES BEFORE.
THR... 333 TIMES...

SIGN: SUPPLIES
THIS FLOOR MAY BE A SAFE POINT, BUT **ANYTHING CAN HAPPEN** IN THE DUNGEON.
ADVENTURERS HAVE ALWAYS ABANDONED THE TOWN IMMEDIATELY WHEN AN IRREGULAR APPEARS, ESCAPING TO THE SURFACE.
THEN, THEY RETURN WHEN THE DUST SETTLES TO REBUILD.
IT'S THE ADVENTURERS' VERY STUBBORNNESS AND AVARICE THAT LED THIS TOWN TO BE CALLED BY MANY...
..."THE MOST BEAUTIFUL ROGUE TOWN IN THE WORLD."
...BIZARRE.
SOMETHING FEELS A BIT OFF.
NOW THAT YOU MENTION IT, THERE'S ALMOST NOBODY AROUND...
IS A TRUE SOMEONE WAS *KILLED*!?
YEAH.
EVERYONE'S GATHERING UP AT WILLY'S!

A MURDER IN TOWN? THAT IS UNUSUAL.
...WHAT SHOULD WE DO, CAPTAIN?
WE WERE PLAN-NING ON GETTING A ROOM HERE.
SO WE CAN'T JUST PRETEND IT'S NOT OUR PROBLEM.
LET'S GO HAVE A LOOK.
ヴィリーの宿
GYA
GYA (RABBLE)
ZAWA
ZAWA (CHATTER)
YEESH— THERE'S NO GETTING THROUGH HERE...
PYON (HOP)
ぴょん
THINK WE!
PYON
ぴょん
CAN GET!
INSIDE THE INN!?
I'LL GO ON AHEAD.
WAIT HERE WITH RIVE-RIA.
CAP-TAIN!? WAIT!!

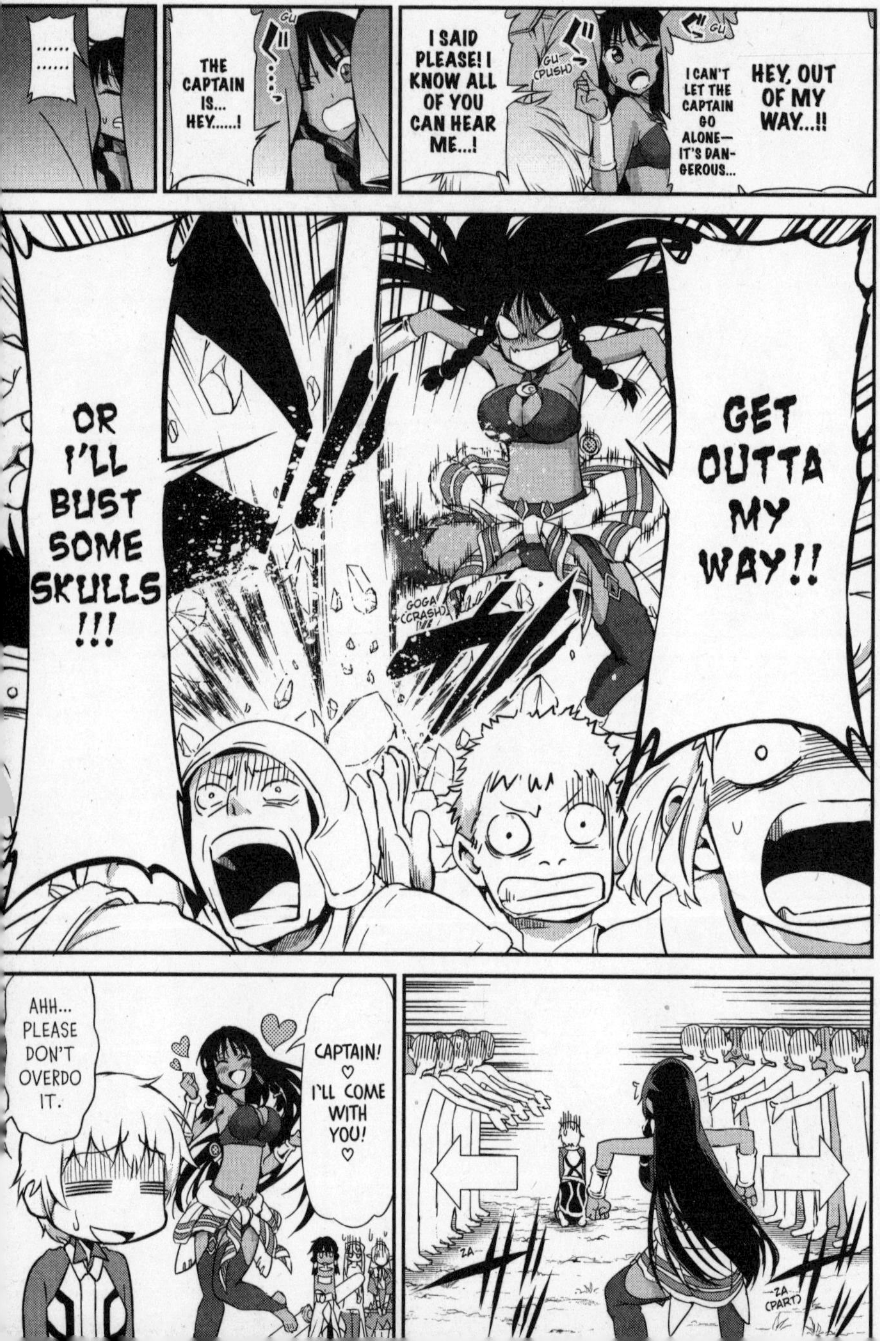
HEY, OUT OF MY WAY...!!
I CAN'T LET THE CAPTAIN GO ALONE— IT'S DANGEROUS...
GU (PUSH)
GU
I SAID PLEASE! I KNOW ALL OF YOU CAN HEAR ME...!
GU
THE CAPTAIN IS... HEY......!
......
......
GET OUTTA MY WAY!!
OR I'LL BUST SOME SKULLS!!!
GOGA (CRASH)
ZA
ZA (PART)
CAPTAIN! ♡ I'LL COME WITH YOU! ♡
AHH... PLEASE DON'T OVERDO IT.

THIS IS...
...YES.
I KNOW IT ALL TOO WELL.
THE SMELL...
...OF SOMETHING THAT USED TO BE HUMAN.

YUCK ...
TALK ABOUT GORY...
THE HELL ARE YOU LOT DOIN' HERE? IT'S OFF-LIMITS!!
ARE MY LOOK-OUTS SLEEP-ING OUT THERE!?
ZUN (FUME)
ZUN
TCH! YOU SURE TALK THE TALK, FINN.
HEY THERE, BORS.
WE'RE PLANNING TO STAY FOR A WHILE.
SO WHY DON'T WE HELP YOU FIGURE THIS OUT AS QUICKLY AS POSSIBLE?
DOESN'T MATTER IF IT'S YOU LOT OR FREYA FAMILIA...
...ALWAYS WALKIN' IN HERE, THINKIN' YOU OWN THE PLACE 'COS YOU'RE STRONG.
BORS ELDER
LEVEL THREE, SECOND-TIER ADVENTURER.
RUNS RIVIRA'S EXCHANGE. THE TOWN'S ACTING LEADER.

RIVIRA IS SELF-GOVERNING, AND THE GUILD HAS NO PRESENCE.
THE TRICK TO KEEPING ROWDY TYPES IN LINE IS BEING STRONG ENOUGH TO KEEP THEM QUIET.
BORS, AT LEVEL THREE, IS THE STRONGEST ADVENTURER IN RIVIRA, AND IS THEREFORE IN CHARGE.
COUGH!
Lv.3
Lv.2
Lv.1
Lv.5
WHAT?
Lv.3
リヴィラの街の食物連鎖
LABEL: RIVIRA'S HIERARCHY
DO WE KNOW ANYTHING ABOUT WHO THE VICTIM IS...
...OR ABOUT THE ATTACKER?
OY, WILLY!
THIS IS YOUR PLACE.
GET YOUR HEAD OUT OF YOUR HANDS AND SPEAK UP!
AH... UM...
THAT GUY OVER THERE WORE FULL-PLATE ARMOR.
COULDN'T SEE HIS FACE BECAUSE OF HIS HELMET.
LAST NIGHT, HE AND A LADY IN A ROBE... COULDN'T SEE HER FACE EITHER, BUT...
...THEY BOTH SHOWED UP AND ASKED ME TO RENT OUT THE WHOLE PLACE.

THE ENTIRE INN TO THEMSELVES?
AHH... THAT'S WHAT THEY HAD IN MIND.
?
BON (BOOM)
!!
YOU GOT IT. AND TAKE A LOOK AT THIS PLACE.
EVEN THE SLIGHTEST MOAN ECHOES FOREVER.
BUT THEY PAID. IF I GET PAID, I GOT NO REASON TO SAY NO.
LEFIYA?
N-N-N-N-NOTHING AT ALL!!
...I STEP OUT FOR THE NIGHT AND COME BACK TO THIS MESS.
WAS A DAMN SHOCK, I TELL YOU.
SO THE GUY BITES THE DUST, AND HIS LADY DISAPPEARS.
SHE'S THE CULPRIT— NO DOUBT ABOUT IT.
AT THE VERY LEAST, SHE KNOWS MORE THAN WE DO.

THIS WOMAN IN A ROBE...
YOU SAID YOU COULDN'T SEE HER FACE, BUT DID SHE HAVE ANY OTHER IDENTIFYING TRAITS?
REMEMBER ANYTHING ABOUT HER PHYSICALLY?
WELL—!
NOW THAT YOU MENTION IT, THAT ROBE COULDN'T HIDE TWO REALLY NICE PHYSICAL TRAITS!!
Ohh! Come to think of it, I saw a lady like that around town yesterday!
RIGHT AROUND HERE.
A real fox, that one! Don't know her face, but that's her!!
JITO (STARE)
じと～
URK!
JIKU (FLINCH)
...IF YOU RUN THIS PLACE...
...HOW DIDN'T YOU HEAR ANYTHING FROM THE FRONT COUNTER?
HE BROUGHT THAT BEAUTY IN HERE AND FLAUNTED HER. I KNEW WHAT WAS UP.
LIKE HELL I'M GONNA STAY HERE WITH THAT GOING ON. I HIT THE BAR RIGHT AWAY.
HAS ANYONE SEEN THIS ROBED WOMAN SINCE LAST NIGHT?
NOPE.
I'VE GOT MY BOYS LOOKIN' INTO IT, BUT NOTHIN' YET.

WH... WHAT ABOUT THE EMBLEM USED TO PAY?
MONEY IS JUST EXTRA BAGGAGE IN THE DUNGEON, SO ADVENTURERS USE THEIR EMBLEMS INSTEAD, RIGHT?
WE COULD LEARN THE VICTIM'S FAMILIA AND THEIR NAME AS THE GUARANTOR IF WE SEE THE PAPERWORK...?
THAT WOULD SURE SPEED THINGS UP...YEAH?
WELL... UM...ABOUT THAT, SORRY. THEY JUST PLOPPED A BAG CRAMMED FULL OF MAGIC STONES ON THE COUNTER...
...AND THAT WAS THAT.
RATS. SO IS THAT AS FAR AS WE GET?
JUST YOU WAIT. WE CAN ASK THIS GUY'S BODY DIRECTLY.
OY! WHERE'S THAT STATUS THIEF!?
BORS-SAN, I GOT IT!!

STATUS THIEF? ISN'T THAT...?
IT IS AN ITEM SOLELY DESIGNED TO REVEAL OUR STATUSES.
'COS SOMETIMES YOU GOTTA BREAK THE RULES.
SHI (DRIP)
STATUS THIEF
ABLE TO RELEASE A DEITY'S "LOCK" AND SHOW A STATUS. AN ILLEGAL ITEM ONLY THOSE WITH THE ADVANCED ABILITY "ENIGMA" CAN PRODUCE. EXTREMELY EXPENSIVE.
THAT GUY DIED LIKE A TOTAL TOOL.
BET YOU ANYTHIN' HE WAS SOME BOTTOM-OF-THE-BARREL PUNK FROM A NO-NAME FAMILIA.
SUU
SUU (SWISH)
ANY OF YOU LOT STUPID ENOUGH TO TAKE ME UP ON IT?
JOB'S DONE, BORS.
LET'S SEE...
SON OF A... FORGOT I CAN'T READ HIERO-GLYPHS....
OY, YOU THERE. GO FIND AN ELF OUTSIDE AND BRING 'EM IN!
WAIT. I AM ABLE TO READ HIERO-GLYPHICS.
ME TOO.

HIS NAME WAS HASHANA DORLIA.
HE BELONGED TO...
...GANESHA FAMILIA.
!!?
GANESHA FAMILIA!? THEY'RE ONE OF ORARIO'S BEST!!
HEY! YOU SURE ABOUT THAT!?
HOLD IT!!

...IS LEVEL FOUR!!
HOLD IT, HOLD IT, HOLD IT! WHAT DID YOU JUST SAY!?
...THIS IS HASHANA!?
THIS AIN'T NO JOKE... THE STRONG FIST WARRIOR HASHANA...

BORS...I NEED TO KNOW.
HAS ANYTHING BEEN MOVED SINCE THE BODY WAS DISCOVERED?
...
WITH NO SIGN OF A FIGHT...
...OR THAT ANYONE ELSE CAME IN...
...THEN THE CULPRIT HAS TO BE AT LEAST LEVEL FOUR...
...OR EVEN A TOP-CLASS ADVENTURER.

THEY COULD BE LEVEL FIVE...
...OR POSSIBLY EVEN STRONGER.

Is it WRONG to TRY to PICK UP GIRLS in a DUNGEON? ON THE SIDE

Sword Oratoria

quest 10. Detectives
Floor eighteen, Rivira, Willy's Inn, the previous night
Hurry up and strip al-ready.
Don't leave me hanging after coming this far.
Easy now, no need to rush.

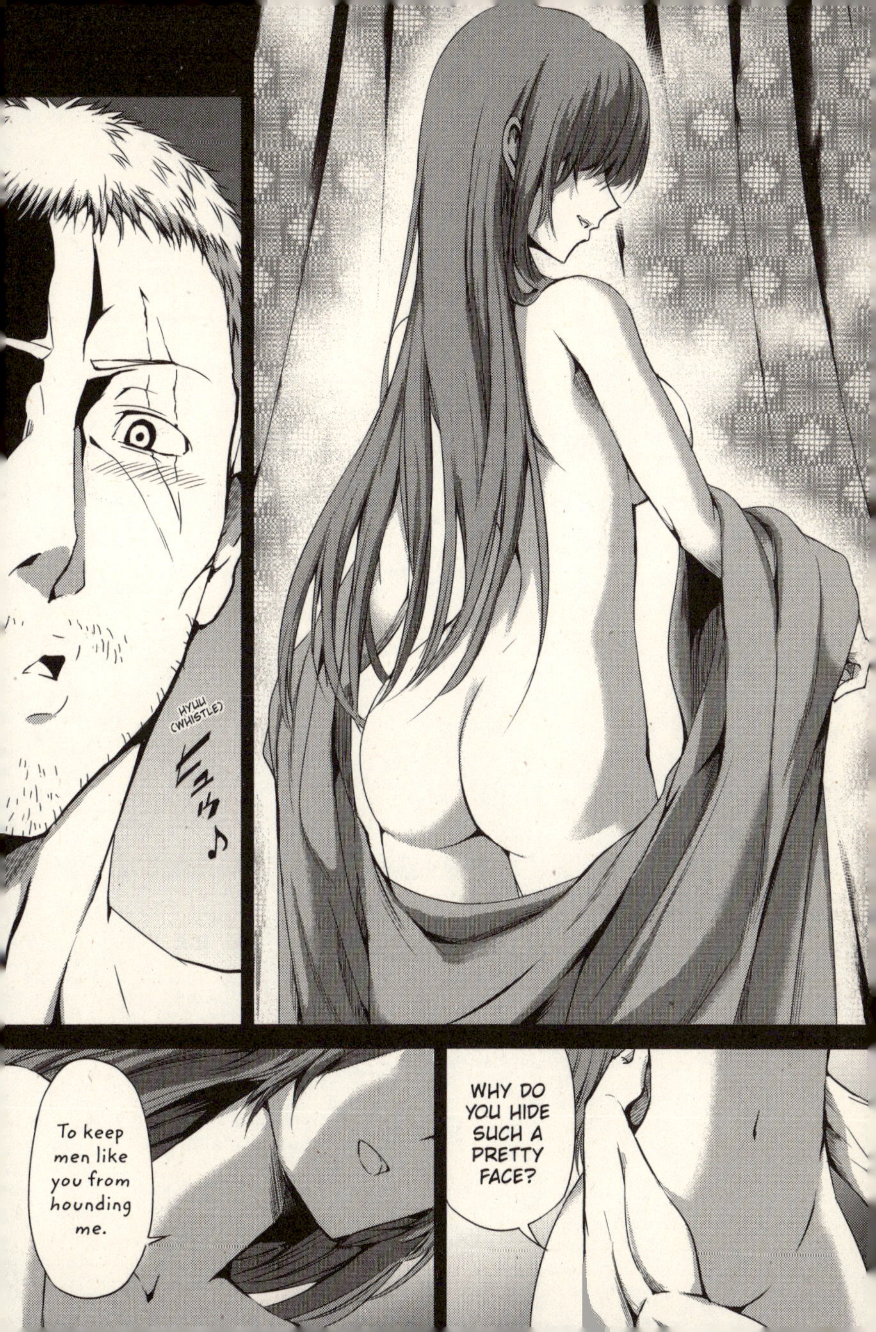
HYUU (WHISTLE)
WHY DO YOU HIDE SUCH A PRETTY FACE?
To keep men like you from hounding me.

We were discussing it before, but what kind of quest did you take?
AHH...... A STRANGE ONE, FOR SURE.
GO TO FLOOR THIRTY, COLLECT SOMETHING WEIRD, AND BRING IT BACK...
OOPS, THAT WAS CLASSIFIED.
PRETEND YOU DIDN'T HEAR IT.
I see ...

GASHI
(GRAB)
GU
(SQUEEZE)
!?
GI
(CRACK)
......
......!?
GA
(CRICK)
GA
GA

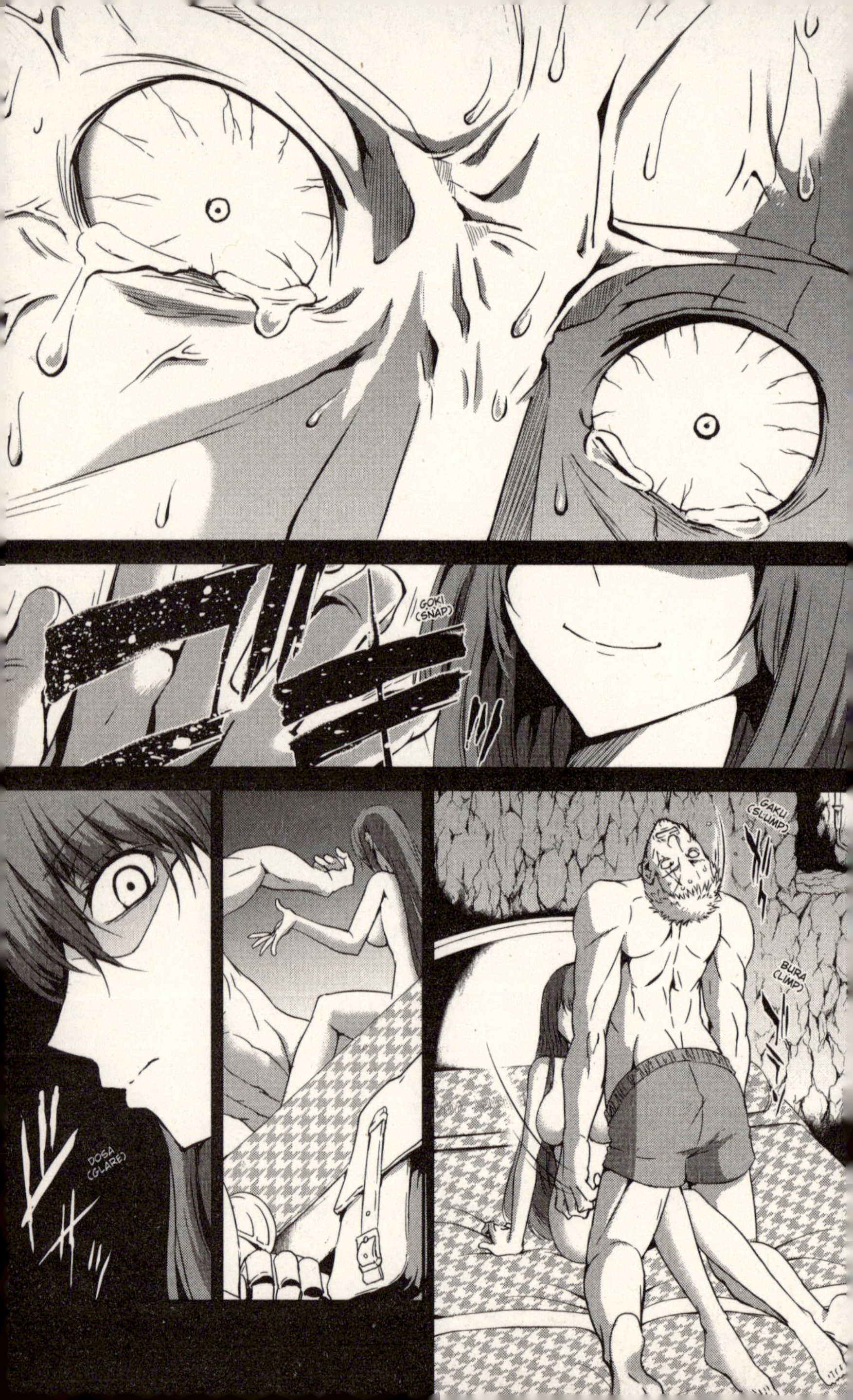
GOKI (SNAP)
GAKU (SLUMP)
BURA (LIMP)
DOSA (GLARE)

GASHA (SLAM)
... Not here.
GIRI (CLENCH)

FLOOR EIGHTEEN, RIVIRA, WILLY'S INN, PRESENT
...IS WHAT I THINK HAPPENED LAST NIGHT.
SO LONG AS I'M NOT OVER-LOOKING ANYTHING.
THE BED IS ALMOST UNTOUCHED... LOOKING AT HASHANA'S BODY, I'D SAY IT HAPPENED BEFORE THEY GOT STARTED.
THINGS IN THIS SMALL ROOM ARE STILL CLEAN AND WHERE THEY SHOULD BE...
...MEANING IT'S UNLIKELY ANYONE ELSE CAME IN HERE.
...SO THAT ROBED WOMAN IS GUILTY AFTER ALL?
OF THAT WE CAN BE SURE.

...D-DID THIS PERSON REALLY MANAGE TO OVERPOWER HIM?
WHAT ... ABOUT POISON?
HASHANA POSSESSED THE "IMMUNITY" ADVANCED ABILITY.
AT "G," EVEN THE MOST POTENT TOXINS WOULD NOT HAVE HAD MUCH EFFECT.
HIS GUARD MAY HAVE BEEN DOWN, BUT THE CULPRIT BROKE A SECOND-TIER ADVENTURER'S NECK.
NECK?
SO SHE BROKE HIS NECK BEFORE SMASHING HIS FACE IN?
MOST LIKELY.
THIS WAS EITHER HER GOAL... OR...
...SHE WAS FRUSTRAT-ED.

THE ROBED WOMAN WAS AFTER SOMETHING THAT HASHANA WAS CARRYING...
...BUT SHE COULDN'T FIND IT.
THEN SHE LOST HER TEMPER AND TOOK IT OUT ON THE CORPSE...?
MAKES SENSE TO ME...
THERE WAS NOTHING USEFUL IN HIS PACK...
...UNFORTUNATELY.
THIS IS ALL I COULD FIND.
PARA (FLAP)
IS THAT...A QUEST REQUEST FORM?
IT'S ALL BLOODY. I CAN'T READ ANY OF IT.
A FEW PLACES ARE STILL LEGIBLE.
"FLOOR THIRTY."
"ALONE."
"RE-TRIEVE."
"SECRET"...
...WITH ALL THIS, WE CAN DEDUCE THAT...

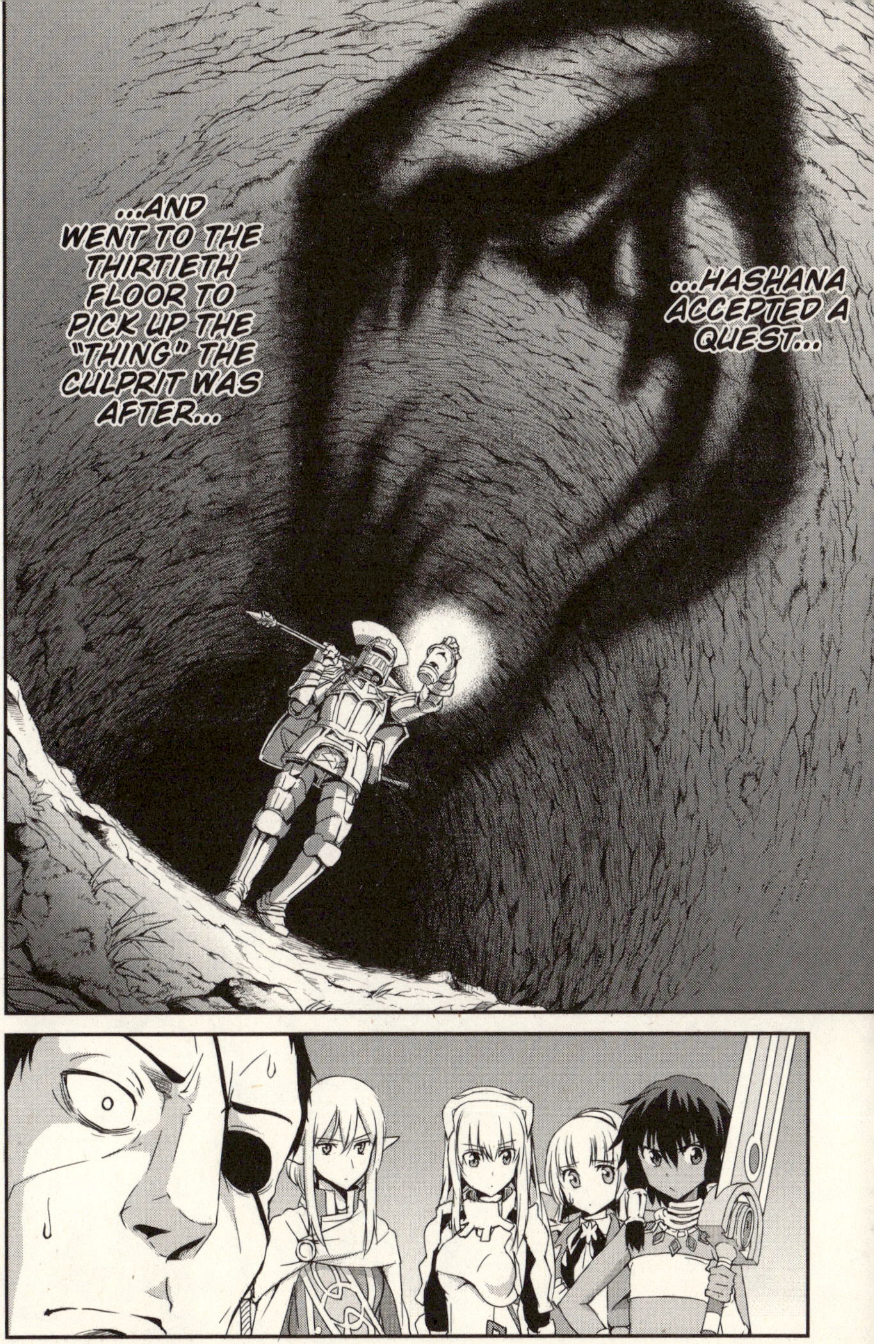
...HASHANA ACCEPTED A QUEST...
...AND WENT TO THE THIRTIETH FLOOR TO PICK UP THE "THING" THE CULPRIT WAS AFTER...

HE PROBABLY DISGUISED HIMSELF AND DIDN'T TELL HIS FAMILIA...
UM... AHH...IT'S TRUE THAT HASHANA ALWAYS WORE A HELMET.
IT HID HIS FACE A LOT, LIKE GANESHA-SAMA'S.
BUT I KNOW FOR A FACT HE NEVER WORE FULL PLATE ARMOR.
Y-YOU'RE TELLING QUITE A CONVINCING STORY, BUT...
...YOU GUYS COULD BE PRETENDING YOU JUST GOT HERE...
...WHEN ONE OF YOU IS ACTUALLY THE KILLER!
HUUH?
I GET IT NOW... THERE AIN'T MANY WOMEN STRONG ENOUGH TO STRANGLE A SECOND-TIER ADVENTURER...
...BUT IF WE'RE TALKING ABOUT THE SCARY FOLKS OF LOKI FAMILIA...

LEAVING FINN OFF THE LIST...
NOT THAT ONE.
AH-HA-HA. NOPE, NOT A CHANCE.
HEY!
WHERE WERE YOU LOOKING WHEN YOU SAID THAT!!?
!
JII (STARE)
...A BODY LIKE THAT COULD LURE ANY MAN SHE WANTED INTO A TRAP, DON'CHA THINK?
PURUN (JIGGLE)
BUCHI (TSK)

!WHAT?
DAN (STOMP)
AS I'VE SAID, I BELONG TO THE CAPTAIN!!
DA HELL WOULD ANY OF YOU KNOW ABOUT IT!!?
ANY FUNNY BUSINESS...
...AND I'LL TEAR YOUR ○×△□ TO SHREDS!!
EEEEK!
KYU
KYU
KYU
KYU (CLASP)

...HAA... BORS...
...THESE WOMEN AREN'T CUT OUT TO MANIPULATE MEN.
I... I SEE. SORRY FOR SUS-PECTIN' YOU.
NOW THAT YOU BELIEVE WE AREN'T INVOLVED IN THIS INCIDENT...
BORS, PLEASE SEAL OFF THE TOWN.
DON'T LET ANY ADVENTURERS STILL IN RIVIRA LEAVE.
SOMEONE OF HASHANA'S CALIBER WAS ASKED TO TAKE ON A SECRET QUEST...
WHATEVER THE CULPRIT WAS AFTER, IT MUST BE EXTREMELY VALUABLE.
I HIGHLY DOUBT SHE WOULD LEAVE HERE EMPTY-HANDED.

I'M PRETTY SURE SHE'S STILL HERE.
...JUST A HUNCH, THOUGH.
GOT IT.
YOU LOT, CLOSE THE NORTH AND SOUTH GATES!
THEN GATHER EVERY ADVENTURER IN TOWN INTO THE SQUARE.
ANYONE WHO GIVES YA FLACK COULD BE THE KILLER— RESTRAIN THEM AT ONCE!!
WELL, THIS ESCALATED QUICKLY.
WE'RE ALREADY INVOLVED, SO LET'S AVENGE HASHANA!
TIME TO CATCH A KILLER!!
...!
LEFIYA?
AH, IT'S NOTHING.

MY HEALED WOUNDS ARE THROB-BING...
AFTER KILLING A MAN AND SCATTERING HIS POSSESSIONS, THE CULPRIT IS STILL HERE DESPITE HER CRIME BEING REVEALED.
HER INSATIABLE DESIRE FOR WHAT SHE SEEKS REMINDS ME...
...OF **THOSE** MON-STERS...
IT'S THE SAME WAY THAT NEW SPECIES CAME AFTER AIZ AND ME BECAUSE OF OUR MAGIC ENERGY.
THIS IS RIVIRA, EIGHTEEN FLOORS DEEP IN THE DUNGEON......
...THERE SHOULD BE NO RELATION TO WHAT HAPPENED ON THE SURFACE...

THE SURFACE, THE LABYRINTH CITY ORARIO
KYA (SQUEE)
KYA
...I HATE WEAK-LINGS. JUST SEEING THEM PISSES ME OFF.
GIRO (GLARE)
TCH!

AHHH, SUCH A WASTE, BETE...
YA GOTTA BE NICE TO THE LADIES, YA HEAR?
PROTECTIN' THE FRAIL DAMSEL IN DISTRESS? DON'T YA'LL ADVENTURERS LOVE THAT STUFF?
HA! MAKES ME WANNA PUKE.
IF YOU CAN'T PROTECT YOURSELF, GO CRAWL IN A HOLE AND DON'T BOTHER COMIN' OUT.
I CAN'T BE THERE TO PROTECT YA FOREVER.
NO STICKIN' YOUR NECK OUT.
...
ANYWAY... THERE'S NOTHIN' I HATE MORE THAN WEAK CHICKS.
I LIKE THE CUTE AND STRONG AIZ.
OTHER GIRLS AIN'T WORTH LOOKIN' AT!
....
OH MY, THE STONE-COLD WOLF IS SUCH A LOVER BOY—!
LIKE. HELL. I. AM—!!?

I KNOW YOU'RE A NICE BOY, BETE.
YA CAN'T FOOL ME.
GH?
I HEARD ALL ABOUT THE RUN-AWAY-MINOTAUR INCIDENT.
HOW YA AND AIZ SAVED ADVENTURERS DOWN THERE.
YOU MAKE A MESS, IT'S YOUR JOB TO CLEAN UP. THAT'S ALL.
SAVING WEAK-LINGS HAD NOTHING TO DO WITH IT.
YEP!
PRICKLY EXTERIOR, BUT HE'S A SOFTY ALL RIGHT!
PWHA-HA-HAAA! SO STOIC, I'M BUSTIN' A RIB OVER HERE.
NGH... KNOCK IT OFF, DAMMIT. PISSING ME OFF...

OY, WASN'T THERE SOMETHING YOU WANTED TO CHECK OUT?
'COS IF NOT, I'M OUTTA HERE.
EASY NOW, HOLD UP.
AFTER THOSE MONSTERS ESCAPED DURING MONSTERPHILIA...
...I TOOK TWO DAYS TO DO SOME DIGGIN' OF MY OWN.
THOSE NEW SPECIES ATTACKED AIZ AND OTHERS.
THEY HURT MY KIDS.
I GOTTA TEACH A CERTAIN SOMEONE...
...WHAT HAPPENS WHEN MY KIDDOS GET HURT.
THAT AIRHEADED VIXEN FREYA LET 'EM LOOSE... BUT...
...THERE'S A SPARE.

WHAT A PAIN... DON'T THE GUILD OR GANESHA'S GUYS KNOW ANYTHING?
THEY WERE TOO BUSY CLEANIN' UP THE FESTIVAL AND TENDIN' TOWNSPEOPLE TO LOOK INTO IT.
GOTTA MAKE SURE I AIN'T OVERLOOKING NOTHIN'.
AND I'M GATHERIN' INFO TO MAKE THAT HAPPEN.
...AND NOW...
...THIS SPOT IS ALL THAT'S LEFT TO CHECK.
GI (CREAK)
HUH? IT'S OPEN.

SFX: BU (SPIT)

SIGN: SEWERS

LOOKS LIKE THE OLD SEWER.
AIN'T THAT FISHY...

OH, COME ON, THIS PLACE IS FLOODED.
BETE, GIMME A RIDE?
GEH?
I DON'T WANNA GET MY SHOES WET!
SO PIGGY-BACK ME—!!
QUIT MESSING AROUND! IT AIN'T THAT DEEP, SO WALK!!
I WON'T GO WITH-OUT A PIGGY-BACK—!!
NOW! ONWARD, BETE!!
PACHI (SMACK)
I WANT A SMOOTH RIDE, YOU HEAR!!?
HEE-HEE-HEE, DO YA FEEL LIKE YOU'RE CARRYIN' A CUTE LITTLE LADY?
TOO BAD, IT'S ME!
JUST SHUT UP.
…… ……
SO, SO? WHAT'S IT LIKE?
WHAT'S IT LIKE TO GIVE ME A PIGGYBACK RIDE RATHER THAN AIZ-TAN!?
WANNA GO FOR A SWIM!!?

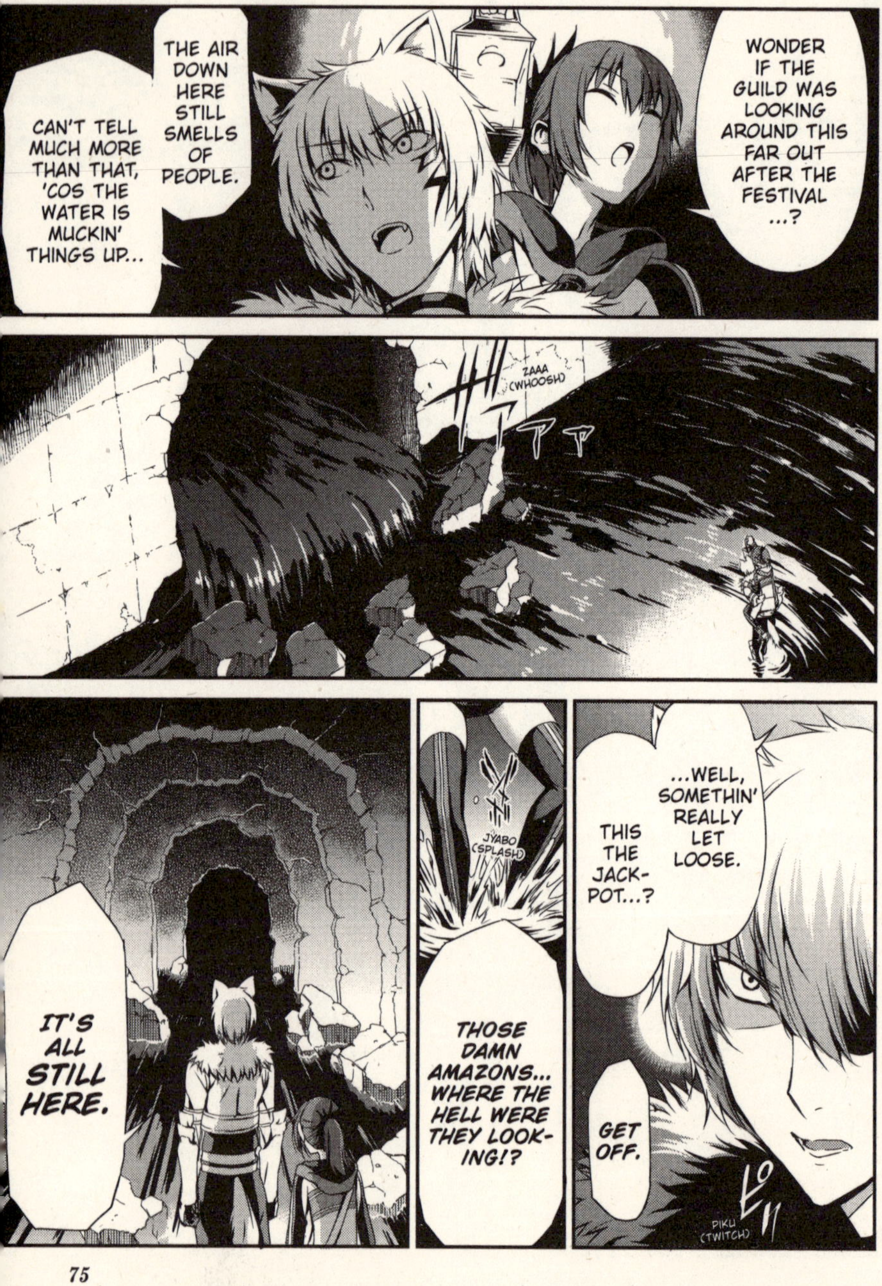
WONDER IF THE GUILD WAS LOOKING AROUND THIS FAR OUT AFTER THE FESTIVAL ...?
THE AIR DOWN HERE STILL SMELLS OF PEOPLE.
CAN'T TELL MUCH MORE THAN THAT, 'COS THE WATER IS MUCKIN' THINGS UP...
ZAAA (WHOOSH)
...WELL, SOMETHIN' REALLY LET LOOSE.
THIS THE JACK-POT...?
GET OFF.
PIKU (TWITCH)
JYABO (SPLASH)
THOSE DAMN AMAZONS... WHERE THE HELL WERE THEY LOOK-ING!?
IT'S ALL STILL HERE.

BASHA (SLOSH)
IS THIS...A RESERVOIR?
ZUZU (SLITHER)
LOKI, GET BACK AND STAY THERE.

DO
(ROAR)
HYU
(LUNGE)
YOU FREAKIN' STINK, ALL OF YOU!!
GYA
(DASH)
GO
(WHAM)

THE HELL YOU NEED THAT SOLID A BODY FOR...!?
GUN (WHOOSH)
WHAT THE —!?
GA
GA
GA (BANG)
MMM ...

GA
GA
GA
GA
GA
GA
GA
GA
...THEY'RE MOVIN' SO FAST I CAN'T TELL WHAT'S HAPPEN-ING...
COULDN'T TELL AT THE FESTIVAL, 'COS THEY WERE STUCK IN THE GROUND, BUT...
...THEY PROBABLY STICK THOSE TAIL-ROOT THINGS INTO THE DUNGEON TO FEED.
BOCHI (SPLAT)
HAAAA (SIGH)
...THAT AIN'T GOOD.

EHGAWD——!!
AAAAHHH-HHHHHH——!!
I'M A GONER! IT'S GONNA CATCH MEEE!?
TCH!!
THERE WAS ANOTHER ONE!?
I...
...WON'T MAKE IT!!!

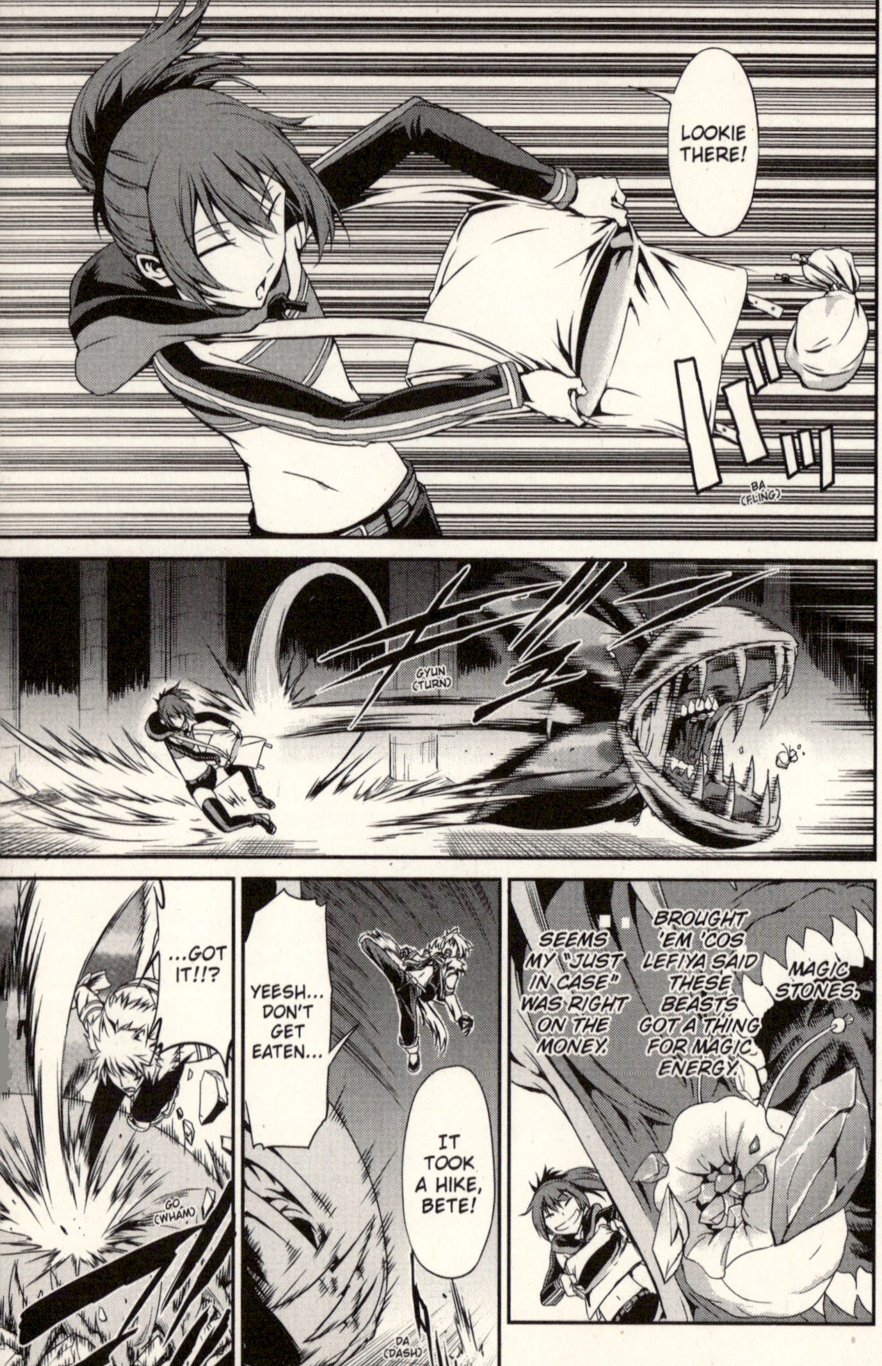
LOOKIE THERE!
BA (FLING)
GYUN (TURN)
MAGIC STONES.
BROUGHT 'EM 'COS LEFIYA SAID THESE BEASTS GOT A THING FOR MAGIC ENERGY.
SEEMS MY "JUST IN CASE" WAS RIGHT ON THE MONEY.
IT TOOK A HIKE, BETE!
YEESH... DON'T GET EATEN...
DA (DASH)
...GOT IT!!?
GO (WHAM)

GACHA (CRASH)
WE MAKE ONE HECKUVA COMBO, BETE! BREATHIN' AS ONE!
GAGAGAGA (SLIDE)
SAY, WERE YA WORRIED ABOUT ME?
WERE YA WOR-RIED?
LIKE HELL I WAS.
TCH... CAN'T EVEN PUT A DENT IN 'EM.
OH YEAH, I HEARD THEY GOT PRETTY THICK SKIN.
AIZ'S SWORD AND LEFIYA'S MAGIC DID THE TRICK, THOUGH.
WHY DIDN'T YOU SAY SO SOON-ER!?
...HATE TO USE IT, BUT WHY NOT?
CHA (SCHICK)
OH! A MAGIC SWORD!

JUST CURIOUS, WHAT DID THAT RUN YA?
ONE MILL.
WHOOOA— A ONE-MILLION-VALIS ATTACK!
THAT'LL BE A SIGHT TO SEE—!
BE SURE TO SNAG ONE OF THEM MAGIC STONES.
BOU (WHOOSH)
MAGIC SWORD
A WEAPON THAT UNLEASHES ENERGY SIMILAR TO A MAGIC SPELL. HOWEVER, ITS USES ARE LIMITED.
EAT THIS!
GOOOO (SWIRL)

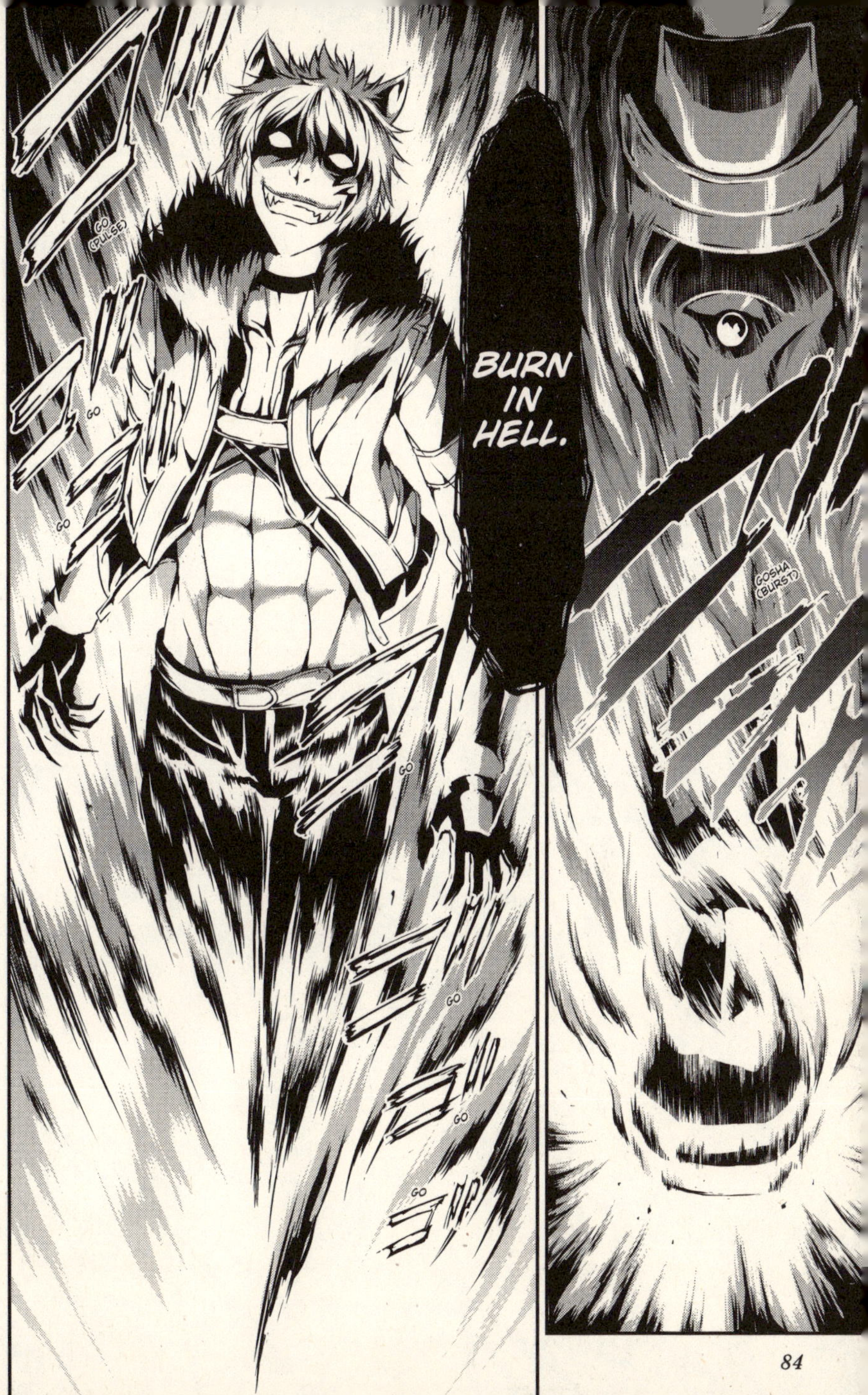
GOSHA (BURST)
BURN IN HELL.
GO (PULSE)
GO
GO
GO
GO
GO
GO

BETE, DID YA KNOW?
THE OPPOSITE OF LOVE IS INDIFFERENCE.
ALL YAR YELLIN' AND SCOFFIN'...
...PROVE YOU CARE FOR THE ONES YOU CALL WEAKLIN'S, EVEN IF IT'S JUST A BIT.
SEEING ME IN A PINCH FLIPPED YAR SWITCH, YEAH?
BUT YA ACT LIKE IT'S A BIG PAIN.
THAT'S WHAT WE DEITIES CALL...
BO (LAUNCH)
...A SOFTY.

I DON'T GIVE A DAMN!!
SEEING WEAKLINGS PISSES ME OFF!
THEY'RE NOTHING BUT DEAD WEIGHT, MAKING THINGS HARD FOR THE STRONG.
CALLING THEM-SELVES ADVEN-TURERS, ACTING ALL TOUGH...
...BUT START BAWLING WHEN THINGS GET DICEY.
PITI-FULLY BEG-GING FOR THEIR LIVES.

GUTLESS WIMPS!!
IF YOU AIN'T GONNA GET UP, GET OUT!!
IF YOU AIN'T GONNA HOWL!...

BURN!!!

...!! YOU DON'T BELONG HERE!!
DOBOA (BOOM)

BO (BOOM)
BETE LOGA, LOKI FAMILIA'S FASTEST LEGS.
HIS QUICK, POTENT ATTACKING STYLE TEARS INTO ENEMIES, RIPPING THEM APART AS IF DEVOURING PREY.
HIS GIVEN TITLE IS...

...CRAZED WOLF "VANARGAND"
ZAAAA (HISSSSS)
...HE SURE CAN LET LOOSE...
ZUUUN (SIZZLE)
DOOO (BURN)
HYUN (ZOOM)
PASHA (SNATCH)
A PROUD LONE WOLF...
THEN AGAIN ...

WAHOO! THE SKY!!
FOUND SOMETHING INTERESTIN', BUT NOTHIN' THAT'LL LEAD US TO THE BAD GUY.
PISHI (FLIP)
HAD TO USE A MAGIC SWORD TOO. WASN'T EVEN WORTH IT.
NOW THAT I GET A GOOD LOOK AT IT, TIONE GOT A MAGIC STONE JUST LIKE THAT FROM A MONSTER ON FLOOR FIFTY.
FIFTY...
PASHA (SNATCH)
YA TALKIN' ABOUT THAT NEW BREED Y'ALL RAN INTO ON THE EXPE-DITION?
YEAH, THAT FILTHY CATERPILLAR MONSTER.
SOMETHING ABOUT THOSE SEWER ONES I JUST FOUGHT REMINDS ME OF IT.

HMM?
YO, DIONY-SUS?
... LOKI?
YO...
HOLD IT.

IT'S THEM.
... WHAT'S THEM?
THAT SMELL I PICKED UP DOWN IN THE SEWERS.
IT WAS THEIRS.

Is it WRONG to TRY to PICK UP GIRLS IN A DUNGEON? ON THE SIDE

Sword Oratoria

quest 11. Red Rum
THAT SMELL I PICKED UP DOWN IN THE SEWER.
IT WAS THEIRS.
...!
DA (STEP)

BA (FWIP)
STAND DOWN, FILVIS. YOU'RE NO MATCH FOR HIM.
BUT...! DIONY-SUS-SAMA!
WE SHALL MAKE NO ATTEMPT TO RUN AND HIDE.
SO WILL YOU NOT HEAR ME OUT, LOKI?
JUST THE TWO OF US IF POSSI-BLE.
...... EH, SURE.
OY, YOU SURE ABOUT THIS?
SHH, IT'LL BE FINE.

I'LL SIGNAL IF THINGS GO SOUR, BETE.
KYAN (SQUEAL)
YOU'LL COME TO MY RESCUE, WON'CHA? ♡
KYAPI
KYAPI (GIGGLE)
......
......
ALL RIGHT.
SPILL THE BEANS.
...OF COURSE...

FIRST, I MUST RESOLVE THE MIS-UNDER-STANDING.
I AM NOT BE-HIND THE INCIDENT, AS YOU SEEM TO BELIEVE, LOKI.
JUST TO CONFIRM, THE INFORMATION YOU SEEK PERTAINS TO THE PLANT MONSTERS, AM I RIGHT?
......YEAH.
I AM ALSO INVESTIGAT-ING THOSE MONSTERS.
WELL, I WAS.
A FEW OF MY FOLLOWERS WERE MURDERED ONE MONTH AGO.
!

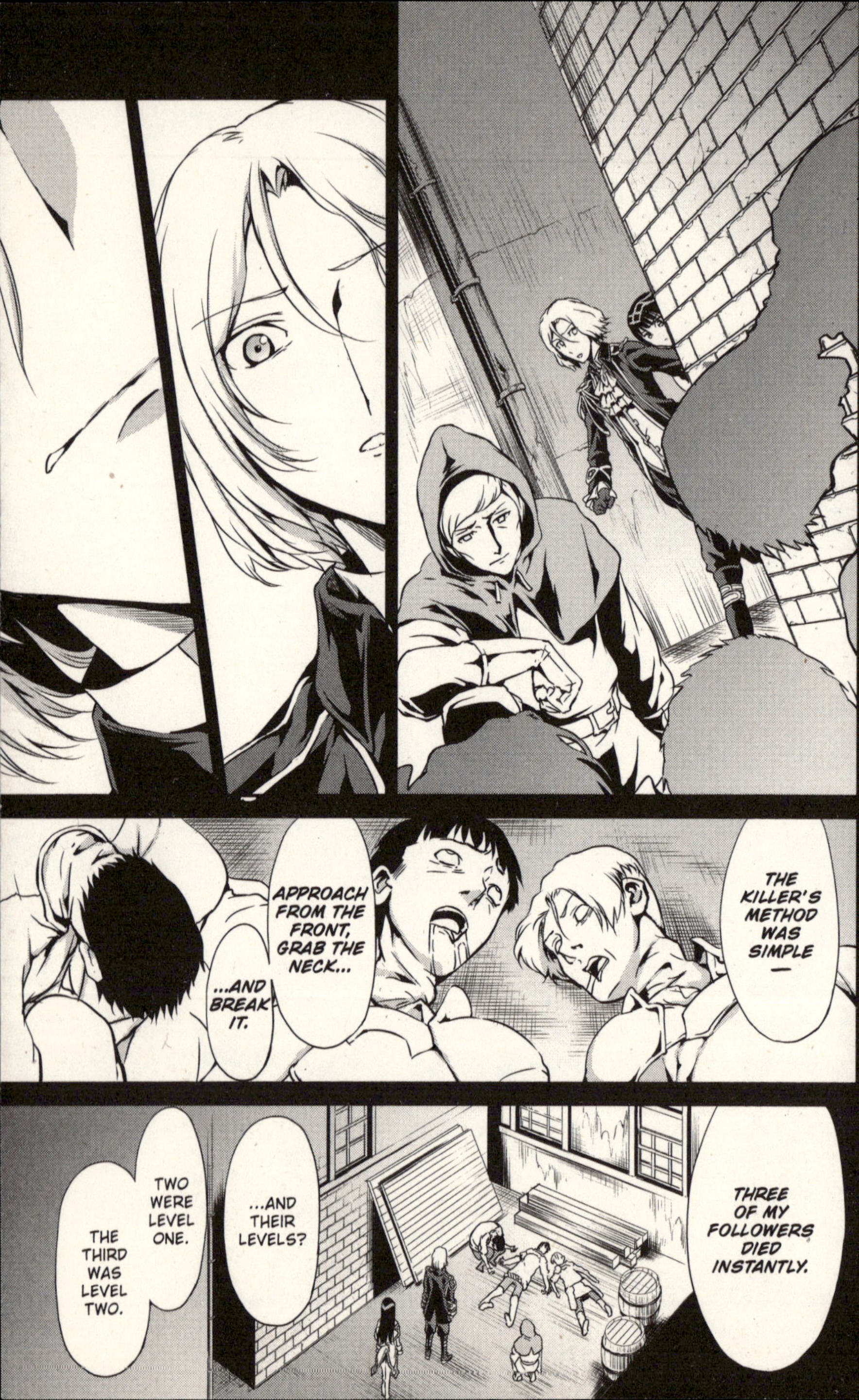
THE KILLER'S METHOD WAS SIMPLE—
APPROACH FROM THE FRONT, GRAB THE NECK...
...AND BREAK IT.
THREE OF MY FOLLOWERS DIED INSTANTLY.
...AND THEIR LEVELS?
TWO WERE LEVEL ONE.
THE THIRD WAS LEVEL TWO.

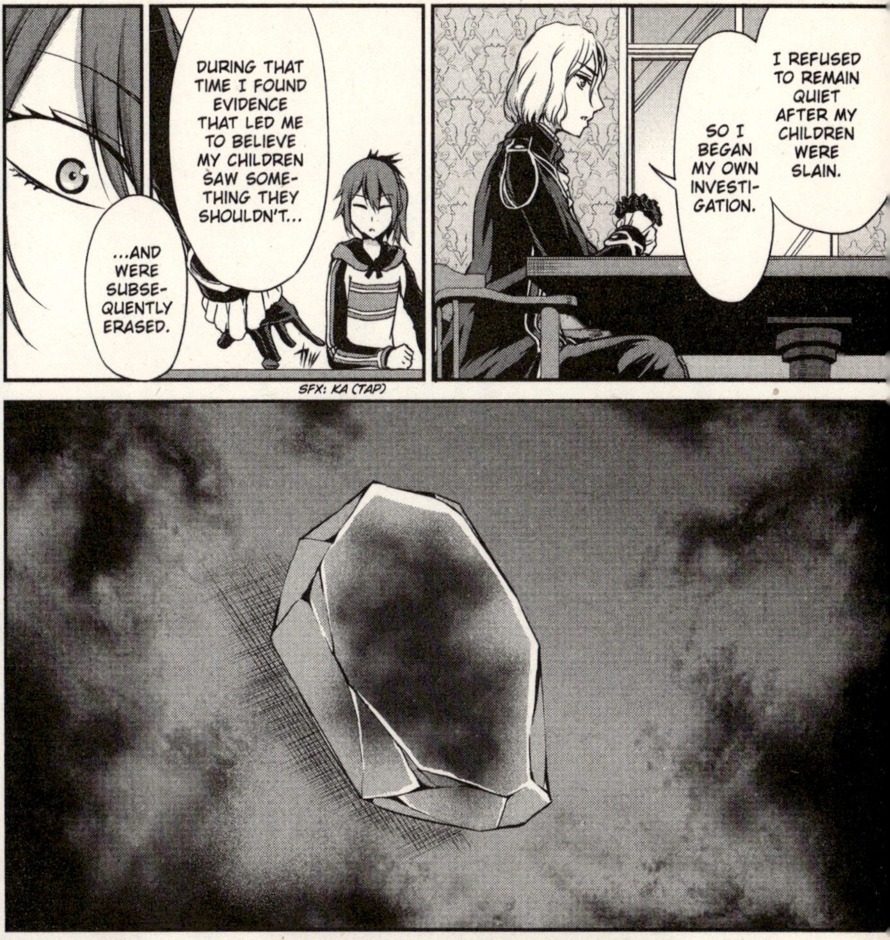
I REFUSED TO REMAIN QUIET AFTER MY CHILDREN WERE SLAIN.
SO I BEGAN MY OWN INVESTIGATION.
DURING THAT TIME I FOUND EVIDENCE THAT LED ME TO BELIEVE MY CHILDREN SAW SOMETHING THEY SHOULDN'T...
...AND WERE SUBSEQUENTLY ERASED.
SFX: KA (TAP)
THIS CAME FROM ONE OF THE MONSTERS YOUR KENKI SLEW ON THE DAY OF MONSTERPHILIA.
I RECOVERED IT BEFORE THE GUILD COULD, YOU SEE.
THE ONE I FOUND ONE MONTH AGO WAS MUCH SMALLER...
...ABOUT THE SIZE OF THE BROKEN SHARD.

SAID SHARD AND MY CHILDREN'S BODIES WERE DISCOVERED IN THE SAME PLACE, A RUN-DOWN ALLEYWAY IN THE CITY'S EASTERN DISTRICT.
RIGHT AROUND THE CORNER FROM WHERE WE ARE NOW.
AND A MAJOR EVENT JUST TOOK PLACE IN THIS AREA.
THE MONSTER-PHILIA...
I HAD A FEELING SOMETHING MIGHT HAPPEN...
...AND SET UP A PERIMETER JUST IN CASE.
WE FOLLOWED THE PLANT MONSTERS INTO THE SEWERS IMMEDIATELY FOLLOWING THE INCIDENT.
THAT IS WHY OUR SMELL WAS PRESENT.
...UNFORTUNATELY, THE MONSTERS WERE TOO STRONG FOR MY CHILDREN TO HANDLE, AND WE WERE FORCED TO ABANDON THE INVESTIGATION WITHOUT ANY CLEAR ANSWERS.

...WELL, I SUPPOSE I'LL TAKE YOU AT YOUR WORD.
I'LL KNOW FOR SURE ONCE I GET TO THE BOTTOM OF THIS ANYWAY.
MY APOLOGIES. THANK YOU, LOKI.
TO TELL YOU THE TRUTH, I WENT TO GANESHA'S BANQUET TO GATHER INFORMATION ON OTHER DEITIES.
SEE IF I COULD FIND ANY SUS-PECTS.
!
GISHI (CREAK)
ARE YOU PLANNING TO STIR UP A RUCKUS?
CHEEKY BASTARD, HE WAS PROVOKING ME...
STEALIN' MAGIC STONES RIGHT OUT FROM UNDER THE GUILD'S NOSE...
FU (SMIRK)
...HE DON'T LOOK IT, BUT HE'S GOT GUTS.
AH! A SMIRK! HOW RARE!

...BUT TO SURPRISE A LEVEL-TWO ADVENTURER HEAD-ON... THAT'S SOMETHIN' ELSE.
THE KILLER MUST BE LEVEL THREE... NO.
AN UPPER-CLASS ADVENTURER, LEVEL FOUR OR THERE-ABOUTS?
YES... I CON-CUR.
KNOWING THAT THE KILLER IS ABOVE LEVEL THREE NARROWS DOWN THE LIST OF PLAUSIBLE FAMILIAS CONSIDER-ABLY.
DON'T FORGET—SOME GODS, LIKE HERMES, DON'T REPORT THEIR KIDS' RANKING UP.
HEY, THERE!
HA-HA-HA...
THAT DANDY'S UP TO THAT KINDA STUFF...?
A CHILD'S LIE IS PLAIN AS DAY TO US DEITIES.
BUT GODS CAN'T TELL IF THEIR OWN KIND'S WORDS RING TRUE.
MANY DEITIES BEND THE RULES.

AS FAR AS I'M CONCERNED, EVERY SINGLE ONE OF THEM IS A SUSPECT...
...AND AN ENEMY OF MY CHILDREN.
SO, WHAT D'YA THINK OF ME?
...YOU ARE INNOCENT, I BE-LIEVE... YES...
...AT THE VERY LEAST, I TRUST YOU MORE THAN ANY OTHER GOD IN ORARIO.
...

...LOKI, HOW DO YOU THINK THOSE PLANT MONSTERS MADE IT TO THE SURFACE?
...ALL SIGNS ARE POINTIN' TO GANESHA.
HIS KIDS BROUGHT UP THE MONSTERS FOR THE FESTIVAL IN THE FIRST PLACE.
BUT THIS IS GANESHA WE'RE TALKING ABOUT. HE LOVES THE KIDS.
IT'S MORE LIKELY A KID WENT ROGUE OR THERE'S SOMEBODY ELSE INVOLVED...
THAT'S NOT IT, LOKI. YOU'RE STARTING FROM FALSE PRETENS-ES.
WHO WAS IT THAT ORDERED GANESHA TO CAPTURE MONSTERS IN THE FIRST PLACE?
EVEN BEFORE THAT...
...WHO WAS IT THAT PLANNED MONSTER-PHILIA TO START WITH?

YOU SAYIN' THE GUILD'S BEHIND EVERY- THING?

HA!
THAT'S CRAZY.
THEY'VE PROTECTED ORARIO'S PEACE, THE GUILD.
WHAT WOULD BE THE POINT?
MONSTER-PHILIA WAS THE GUILD'S IDEA.
NOT THE ECCENTRIC GODS...
...BUT THE GUILD.
AND RELATIVELY RECENTLY.
OUT OF THE BLUE.
WITH NO EXPLA-NATION TO SPEAK OF.
OTHER DEITIES AGREED IT "SOUNDS INTERESTING" AT DENATUS...
...AND APPROVED THE PLAN WITHOUT FURTHER INQUIRY.

I HAVE A SUGGES-TION...
...?
SU (SHF)
WOULD YOU BE WILLING TO INVESTIGATE THE GUILD FOR ME?
HUH !?
SHOULD THE GUILD HAVE ANYONE ABOVE LEVEL THREE...
IF OURANOS HAS WARRIORS UNDER HIS COMMAND, IT'D BE TOO MUCH FOR MY CHILDREN TO HANDLE.
ON THE OTHER HAND, AS LEADER OF ONE OF THE STRONGEST FAMILIAS IN ORARIO, YOU DON'T HAVE THAT PROBLEM, DO YOU?
QUIT HORSIN' AROUND !!
WHO WOULD ACTUALLY DO SOMETHIN' THAT BONE-HEADED!?
GAN (SLAM)

YOU CAN'T PRETEND NONE OF THIS EVER HAPPENED EITHER, NOW CAN YOU, LOKI?
!
...YOU PLANNED ON DRAGGIN' ME INTO THIS FROM THE START, DIDN'T YOU?
GURURURU (GRIND)
A COINCI-DENCE, I ASSURE YOU.
BUT YES, I DID INTEND TO LOOK FOR SOME ASSISTANCE.
WE SHALL CONTINUE OUR OWN INVESTIGA-TION.
PLEASE GIVE IT SOME THOUGHT.

OY, YOU FINISHED YET?
TCH!
DAN (STOMP)

SORRY, BETE. COULD YA STICK WITH ME A BIT LONGER?
......

THE GUILD.
THE LARGE GOVERNING ORGANIZATION THAT MANAGES THE LABYRINTH CITY ORARIO.
THEY REGISTER CITY CITIZENS AS ADVENTURERS, SUPPLY ALL TYPES OF DUNGEON-RELATED INFORMATION TO THE PUBLIC...
...HARNESS THE BENEFITS OF THE DUNGEON BY EXCHANGING MAGIC STONES AND DROP ITEMS FOR MONEY, AND PROVIDE DUNGEON PROWLING SUPPORT.
THEY ARE COMPLETELY IN CHARGE OF THE DUNGEON AND EVERYTHING CONNECTED TO IT.
A VITAL COMPONENT TO LIFE AS AN ADVENTURER.
ALTHOUGH A DEITY OVERSEES THE GUILD, NONE OF ITS EMPLOYEES ARE BLESSED WITH FALNA.
THEREFORE, THEY ARE NOT A FAMILIA...
...NOR CAN THEY USE FORCE.
...AND THAT'S HOW IT IS.
HUH? DID YOU SAY SOMETHING?

BETE, IF I AIN'T BACK IN AN HOUR...
...SOMETHIN' PROBABLY HAPPENED TO ME, SO FEEL FREE TO CHARGE IN.
COUNTIN' ON YA.
NOW, I WONDER WHAT I'M GONNA FIND...

OH!
LOKI-SAMA!
HI, MISHA-CHAN. WORKIN' HARD, I SEE.
TOTETETETE (TROT)
MISHA FROT
AN ADVENTURER ADVISER WHO HANDLES PAPERWORK AND OTHER SMALL JOBS, SHE IS ONE OF THE GUILD'S RECEPTIONISTS. GUILD RECEPTIONISTS ARE KNOWN FOR THEIR BEAUTY...
CAN I HELP YOU WITH SOMETHING TODAY?
YEAH, YA CAN.
I GOT SOMETHIN' I WANNA ASK.
KOKKUN CLEAN
KOKKUN
IS OURANOS AROUND?
PISHI (ZING)

GIGIGI (TREMBLE)
O-O-O-OURANOS-SAMA!?
UH, UM, WELL...
NO, NO, MISHA-CHAN.
EVERY-BODY'S BUSY, SO YA GOTTA DO YOUR JOB.
GASHI (GRAB)
SEE THAT? LOKI IS HITTING ON ANOTHER RECEPTIONIST.
JUST LEAVE THEM BE. HAPPENS ALL THE TIME.
...!!
SORRY, MISHA! PLEASE TAKE ONE FOR THE TEAM. I'M TOO BUSY FOR THIS.
NOW THEN, MISHA-CHAN. CAN'T YA ANSWER ONE LITTLE QUESTION?
UM...
A-AND THAT IS...?
OURANOS IN HIS USUAL SPOT?
GIKUN (SHUDDER)
...!

THANKS, MISHA-CHAN. DRINKS ARE ON ME NEXT TIME.
SUTATATA (ZIP)
L-LOKI-SAMA!?
YO!
SUI (ZOOM)
HUH?
WHAT??
KEEP UP THE GOOD WORK.
SURU (WEAVE)
SURU
IF MEMORY SERVES ME RIGHT, THIS SHOULD BE THE WAY...
DOWN THIS HALL, MAYBE?
HM...? COMPANY?
PLEASE STOP, GODDESS LOKI!?
BATA
BATA
BATA
BATA (TMP)

YO, ROYMAN. LONG TIME NO SEE.
HOW YA BEEN?
G-GODDESS LOKI. THIS IS A SACRED PATH THAT LEADS TO THE TEMPLE OF OURANOS.
HAA... HAA.
HAA.
PLEASE TURN BACK!
ROYMAN MARDEEL
THE GUILD'S HIGHEST RANKING OFFICIAL. A MIDDLE-AGED ELF WHO IS REFERRED TO AS THE "GUILD'S PIG" BY HIS OWN KIND FOR HIS LUXURIOUS LIFESTYLE.
WELL, I'LL BE! PUT ON MORE WEIGHT, HAVE YA?
WHAT IS THE MEANING OF GRABBING ME LIKE THIS...!!?
YOU'RE ALL SQUISHY.
BUNI (JIGGLE)
GOD-DESS LOKI!
THE GUILD IS AN INDEPENDENT ENTITY. EVEN YOUR POSITION AS A GOD DOES NOT ALLOW YOU ENTRY...!
たぷ たぷ たぷ たぷ たぷ たぷ たぷ たぷ
TAPU (TAP)
DON'T BE SUCH A STICK IN THE MUD.
I JUST WANNA ASK OURANOS SOMETHIN'.

ROYMAN... INVESTIGATIN' THE GUILD WOULD START WITH INVESTIGATIN' HIM, BUT...
PYON (PULL)
...WELL, "THIS" LITTLE PIGGY IS PROBABLY CLEAN.
YOU MUST NOT GO! ABSO-LUTELY NOT!!
WHEN IT COMES DOWN TO IT...
BUT THEN, THIS TRIP IS JUST TO...
THEN AGAIN, IF THEY DON'T LET ME PASS...
WHAT TO DO, WHAT TO DO...
—IT IS NO MATTER. ROYMAN, LET HER PASS.
BUT, OURA-NOS ...!
I SAID IT IS NO MATTER. ALL OF YOU, LEAVE US.
!!

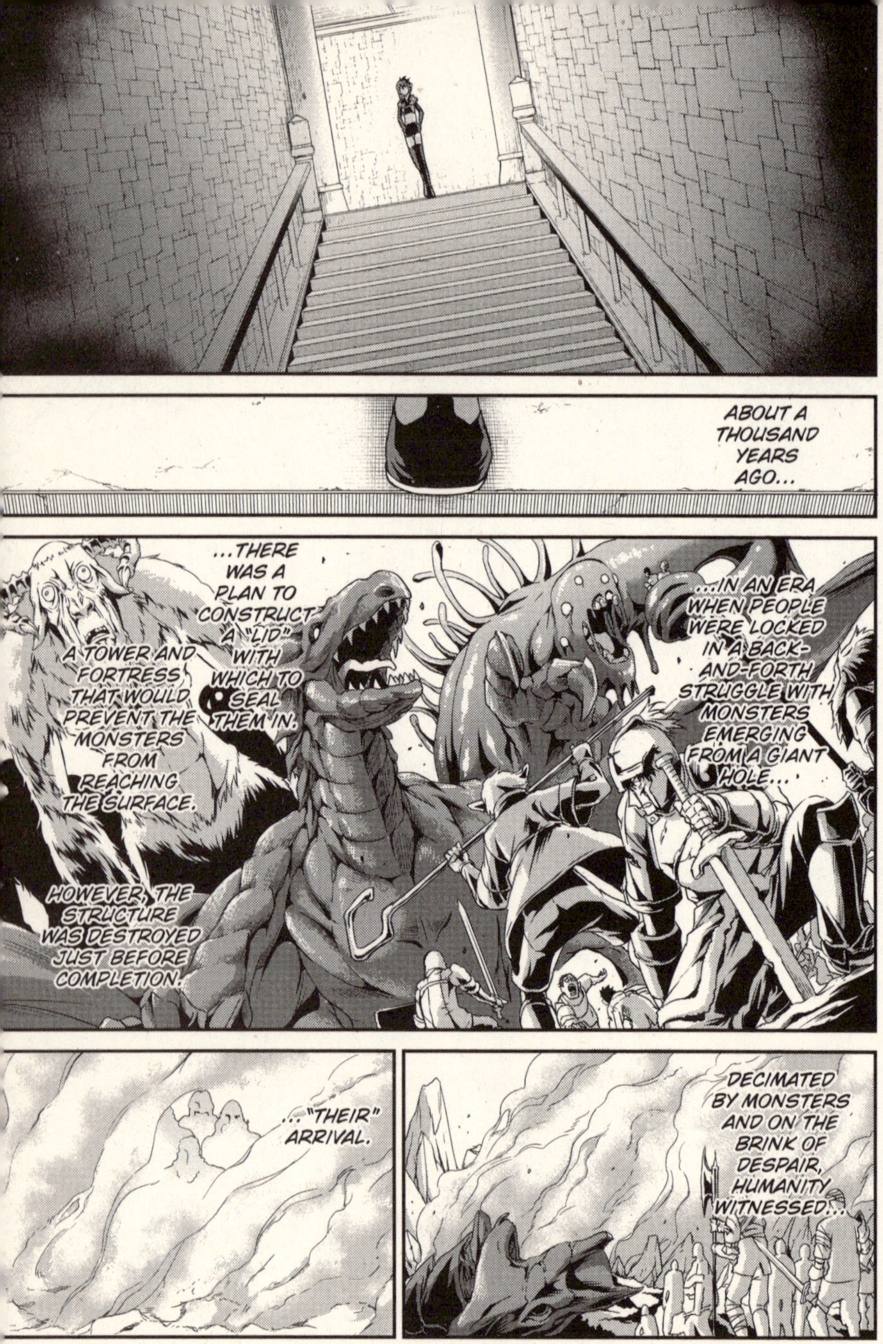

ABOUT A THOUSAND YEARS AGO...
...IN AN ERA WHEN PEOPLE WERE LOCKED IN A BACK-AND-FORTH STRUGGLE WITH MONSTERS EMERGING FROM A GIANT HOLE...
...THERE WAS A PLAN TO CONSTRUCT A "LID" WITH WHICH TO SEAL THEM IN.
A TOWER AND FORTRESS THAT WOULD PREVENT THE MONSTERS FROM REACHING THE SURFACE.
HOWEVER, THE STRUCTURE WAS DESTROYED JUST BEFORE COMPLETION.
DECIMATED BY MONSTERS AND ON THE BRINK OF DESPAIR, HUMANITY WITNESSED...
..."THEIR" ARRIVAL.

遊びに来た。
WE CAME FOR A GOOD TIME.
ポカーーーン
POKAN (SHOCK)
AMID THE DEITIES WANTING TO BE "ENTERTAINED"...
ゾロ ゾロ
ZORO ZORO (GLANCE)
...ONE GOD WAS DIFFERENT.

OURANOS, THE FATHER OF ORARIO.

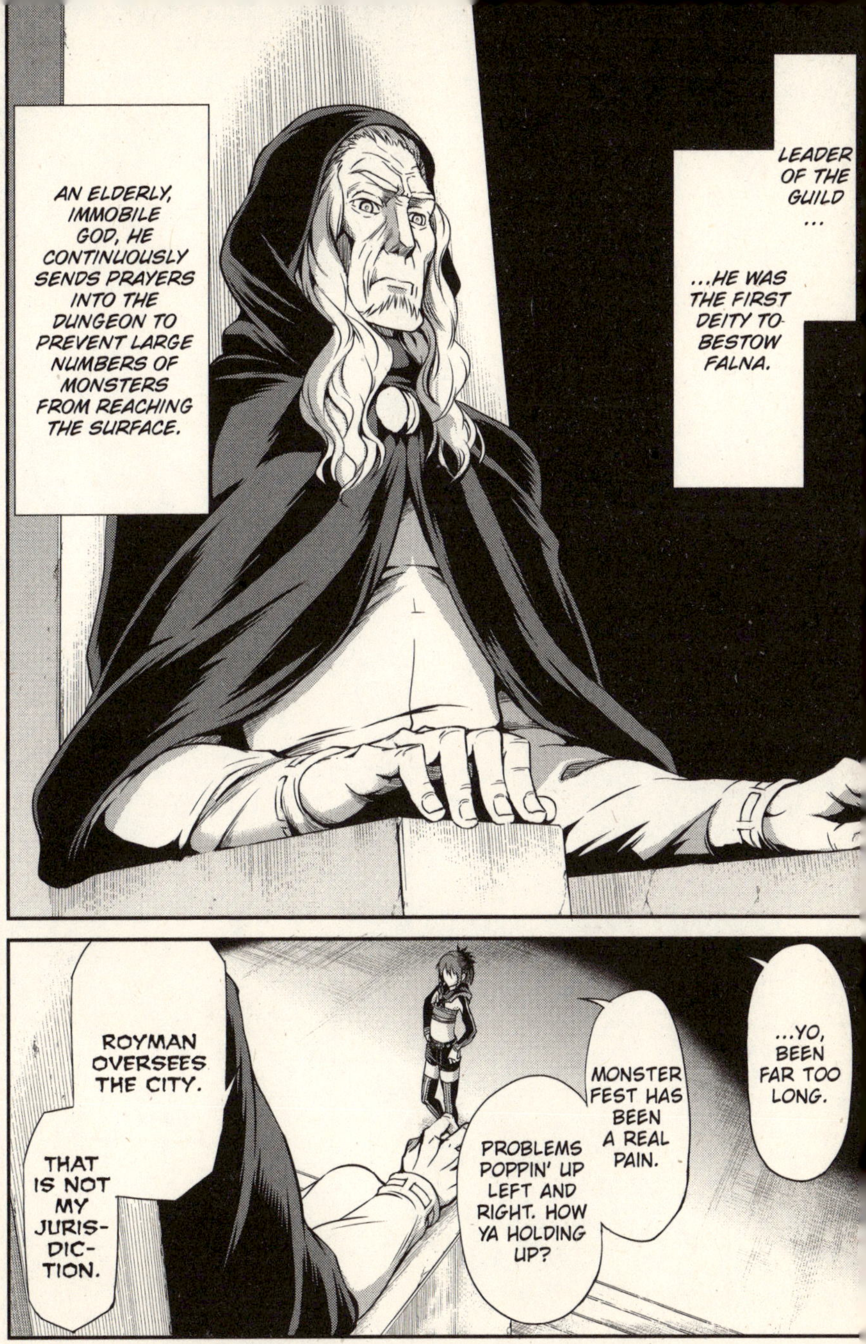
LEADER OF THE GUILD ...
...HE WAS THE FIRST DEITY TO BESTOW FALNA.
AN ELDERLY, IMMOBILE GOD, HE CONTINUOUSLY SENDS PRAYERS INTO THE DUNGEON TO PREVENT LARGE NUMBERS OF MONSTERS FROM REACHING THE SURFACE.
...YO, BEEN FAR TOO LONG.
MONSTER FEST HAS BEEN A REAL PAIN.
PROBLEMS POPPIN' UP LEFT AND RIGHT. HOW YA HOLDING UP?
ROYMAN OVERSEES THE CITY.
THAT IS NOT MY JURIS-DIC-TION.

THIS YEAR'S MON-STER FEST WAS A REAL DOOZY.
THESE NASTY, SLITHERY MONSTERS SHOWED UP TOO.
NOW, HOW DID THEY GET UP HERE?
AND WHO ORDERED THEM TO DO IT? WISH I KNEW...
WHO'S PULLING THE STRINGS TO THOSE PLANT MONSTERS?
THE GUILD?

PACHI (CRACKLE)
IT IS NOT...
... AS YOU SAY.
...THAT SO?

SORRY TO BARGE IN ON YA. KEEP DOIN' WHAT YOU'RE DOIN'.
PRETTY SURE SOMEBODY'S BEEN WATCHING ME THE WHOLE TIME...
...BUT, EH, DON'T CARE.
TRUSTING OURANOS SHOULD BE FINE.
SOUNDS LIKE HE'S INVOLVED IN SOMETHING ELSE, BUT...
...DIONYSUS'S HUNCH MUST BE OFF.
THERE COULD BE SOMETHING GOIN' ON IN THE GUILD UNDER OURANOS'S NOSE.
MANY DEITIES BEND THE RULES.
VERY TRUE...

SOME-THING'S ABOUT TO HAPPEN IN ORARIO.
ON THE STAGE FULL OF CLOWNS...
...A BLOOD-RED CLOWN IS SMILIN'.
AHH...

THIS IS WHY EARTH IS SO INTER-ESTING.
ZAWA (CHATTER)
ZAWA

DUNGEON, FLOOR EIGHTEEN, TOWN OF RIVIRA
ZAWA ZAWA (CHATTER)
THAT DIDN'T TAKE LONG.
KUI KUI (MUTTER)
'COS I THREATENED TO BLACK-LIST ANYONE WHO DIDN'T SHOW.
AND BEING ALONE RIGHT NOW WOULD BE... FRIGHTENING.
I THOUGHT GETTING EVERYONE IN ONE PLACE WOULD MAKE FINDING TOP-CLASS ADVENTURERS OTHER THAN YOU LOT EASIER, BUT...
THE CULPRIT MOST LIKELY WANTED TO MAKE A SCENE FROM THE START.
BE IT A DISGUISE OR CON-CEALING THEIR TRUE LEVEL...
THEY SURELY HAVE ONE OR TWO SAFE-GUARDS IN PLACE.
WE AIN'T DEALING WITH AN IDIOT.

AW MAN, DO WE GOTTA CHECK EEEVERY-ONEEE?
NO. WE KNOW IT WAS A WOMAN WHO ATTACKED HASHANA, SO...
OH, THAT'S RIGHT! WE JUST HAVE TO CHECK THE FEMALE ADVENTURERS!
COULD YOU BE ANY SLOWER ...?
TO BE MORE PRECISE, JUST THE ONES WITH A SIMILAR BODY SHAPE TO TIONE-SAN.
WHAT IS THE MATTER, FINN?
YOU LOOK TROUBLED DESPITE OUR PROGRESS.
....

PROG-RESS... SHOULD NOT BE THIS EASY.
...HOW DO YOU MEAN?
WE SPLIT INTO THREE GROUPS...
...TO HELP GATHER EVERY-ONE HERE.

AIZ AND LEFIYA PROTECTED THE NORTH GATE.
TIONA AND TIONE GUARDED THE SOUTH.
ALL THE WHILE...YOU AND I WERE HERE, IN THE MIDDLE OF TOWN...
...TO MAKE SURE EVERY-ONE SAW US.
OUR NAMES AND FACES ARE WELL KNOWN, EVEN OUTSIDE ORARIO.
OUR ABILI-TIES AS WELL.
EVEN IF THE CULPRIT IS AS STRONG AS AIZ, ANY ONE OF US COULD CAPTURE HER.
EVEN MORE SO WITH SIX OF US TO-GETHER.
!
...IF THE CULPRIT IS AWARE OF THAT AS WELL...
IN OTHER WORDS ...

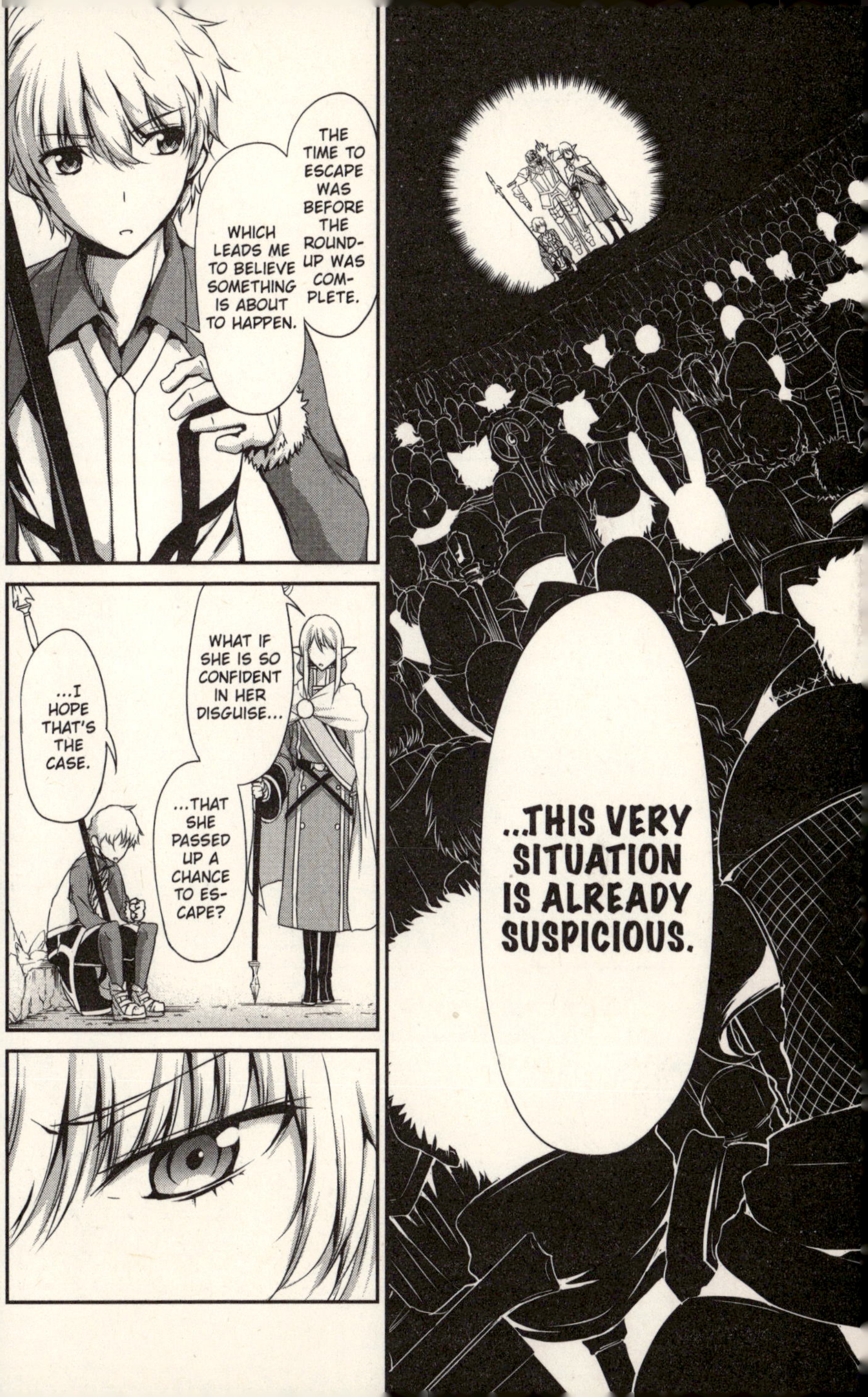
THE TIME TO ESCAPE WAS BEFORE THE ROUND-UP WAS COM-PLETE.
WHICH LEADS ME TO BELIEVE SOMETHING IS ABOUT TO HAPPEN.
WHAT IF SHE IS SO CONFIDENT IN HER DISGUISE...
...THAT SHE PASSED UP A CHANCE TO ES-CAPE?
...I HOPE THAT'S THE CASE.
...THIS VERY SITUATION IS ALREADY SUSPICIOUS.

MY THUMB WON'T STOP SHAKING...
WHAT...? WHAT AM I MISSING?
IT'S LIKE A JIGSAW PUZZLE THAT'S MISSING A PIECE.
WHY DOES SOMETHING FEEL WRONG...?

WE'RE... DOING AN INVESTIGATION, RIGHT?
IT WOULD SAVE A LOT OF TIME TO CHECK EVERYONE'S STATUS AND LEVEL ONE BY ONE, BUT...
...THAT WOULD VIOLATE THE RULES AND PISS OFF EVERY FAMILIA IN THE CITY.
YOU GOT THAT RIGHT.
WELP, LOOKS LIKE WE GOT NO CHOICE...
ALL RIGHT LADIES, LISTEN UP!! OFF WITH YOUR CLOTHES—!

WE'RE CHECKING BODIES AND BAGS!!
YOU HAVE TO SHOW US EVERY SINGLE INCH—!!
BOOOO
HUH!?
SERIOUSLY!?
PERVERTS!
BOOOOOO
DON'T BE FOOL-ISH.
WE WILL BE CONDUCT-ING THE INVESTIGA-TION.
YEEEEP!
YES.
I SHALL CON-TRIBUTE.
MEN, I SWEAR.
PLEASE LINE UP...
...HERE...

FINN, SEARCH ME, PLEASE!
UM, I'M YOUR BIGGEST FAN!!
......
ZURA (CROWD)
Pretty please!
KYA (SQUEE)
KYA
Every single inch, twice!!
STOP, TIONE!!
MISHI (TWITCH)
DAMN THOSE SLUTS ...!!
GET YOUR HANDS OFF ME!!
CAN'T YOU SEE THEY'RE JUST PERVERTED PIG SOWS LUSTING OVER A STRONG, HOT YOUNG MAN!!?
ZURI (YANK)
ZURI
SOME-BODY BRING HER A MIR-ROR!
ZURI
ZURI
BUT NONE OF THEM HAVE ANY CLUE!!
THE CAPTAIN! IS ALMOST FORTY!! AND HAS ELEGANCE ACHIEVED WITH MATURITY!!!
EVERY-ONE, RUN AWAY! SOME-THING BAD IS COMING!!
HFF! HFF!

FINN IS GETTING SMOTH-ERED—!
KYA
KYA
NO, THEY ARE DRAG-GING HIM AWAY—!!
DO
DO (TMP)
DO
DO
OVER MY DEAD BODY!!
SOME-THING ALREADY DID HAP-PEN...
NHH ...
DON (WHAM)
BON (FLING)
WELL... UM...
HAA...
I DON'T KNOW WHAT'S GOING ON ANY-MORE ...
...?

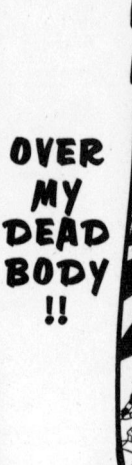

JIRI (STEP)
BA (DASH)
!!
THAT GIRL...!!
LET'S GO.
TA (JUMP)
EH !?
AH...Y-YES!!

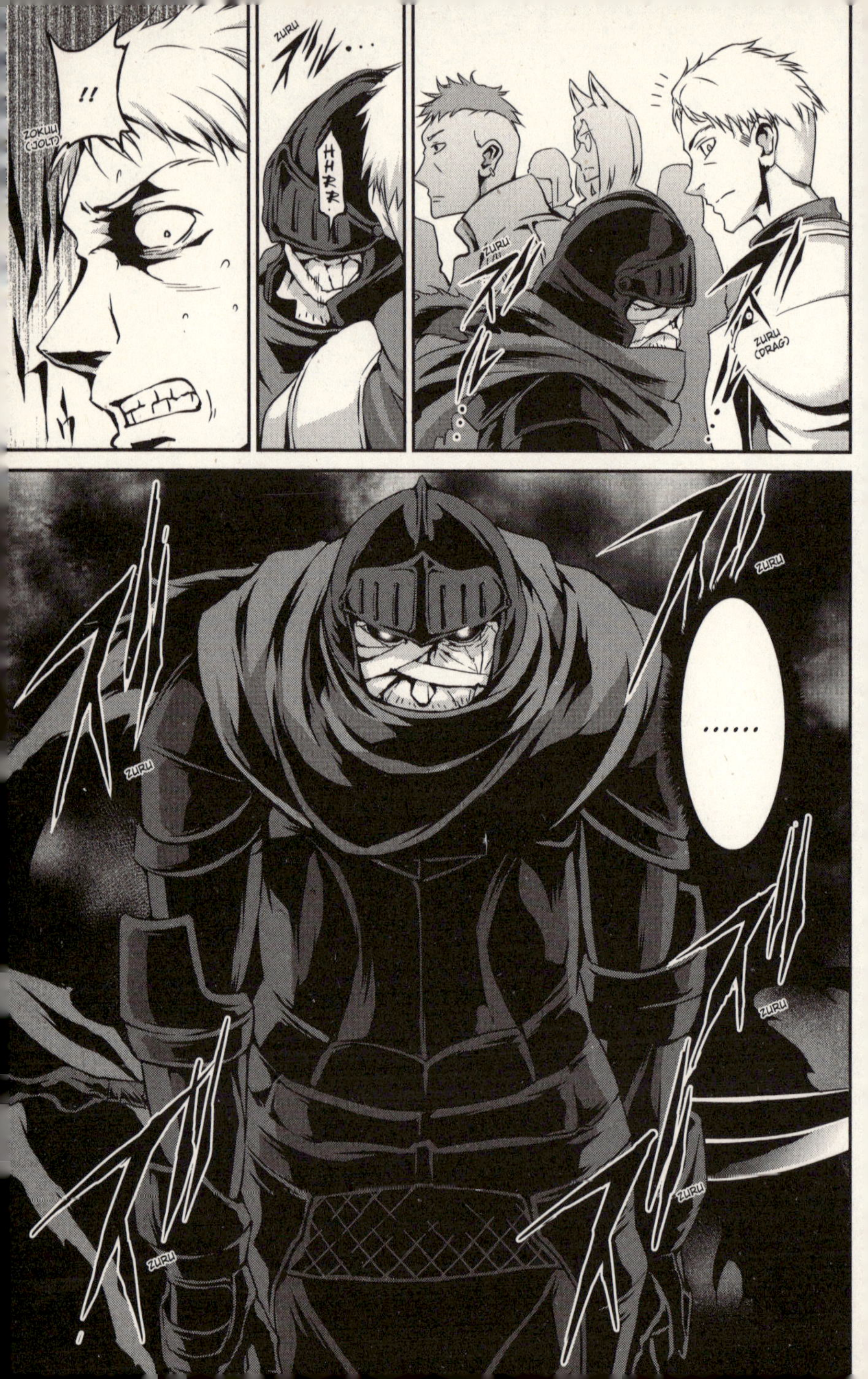
!!
ZOKUU (JOLT)
ZURU
HHRR.
ZURU
ZURU (DRAG)
ZURU
......
ZURU
ZURU
ZURU
ZURU

Is it WRONG to TRY to PICK UP GIRLS IN A DUNGEON? ON THE SIDE

Sword Oratoria

quest 12. Unknown

POU (GLOW)
TA (THUMP)
TA
TA
TA
TA
TA
TA
HAA!
HAA!
HAA!
!?
WEREN'T THERE TWO OF THEM?
THEY'RE... STILL COMING!!

ZUTA (THUD)
EEEEH!!?
HFF.
HFF.
HENA (CRUMPLE)
HENA
HENA...
PETA (PLOP)
HAA...
TH...THE PINCER FORMATION WORKED PERFECTLY.
YOU'RE AMAZING, AIZ-SAN...!
HAA...
NOT REALLY. IT WORKED BECAUSE YOU PUSHED YOURSELF, LEFIYA.
ESCAPEE
FULL SPEED
WARP SPEED
IT MIGHT BE BETTER FOR THE OTHERS TO ASK HER QUESTIONS, RATHER THAN US.
I AGREE. LET'S GO BACK TO THE SQUARE.
!!

PLEASE, NO! IF I GO BACK THERE, THEN THIS TIME I'LL...!
SURELY, I'LL BE ...!!
!
NO !!
PLEASE... PLEASE...
WHAT... SHOULD WE DO...?
......
......

THERE'S NO ONE HERE, SO WILL YOU PLEASE TELL US WHAT'S GOING ON?
... OKAY.
WHAT'S YOUR NAME?
LULUNE... LULUNE LOUIE.
WOULD YOU TELL US YOUR LEVEL AND FAMILIA?
THIRD TIER, LEVEL TWO. HERMES FAMILIA.
WHY DID YOU RUN AWAY FROM THE SQUARE?
......BE-CAUSE I THOUGHT SOMEONE WAS GOING TO KILL ME.
WHY DID YOU THINK THAT?
...
...WAS IT...
...BECAUSE YOU'RE CARRY-ING SOMETHING THAT BELONGS TO HASHANA-SAN?
BIKU (FLINCH)
!!

WH-WHY WOULD YOU BE CARRYING THAT...!?
I-IT'S NOT WHAT YOU THINK!! I JUST...!
...I ACCEPTED A QUEST...
...TO COME DOWN HERE, PICK UP A PACKAGE, AND BRING IT BACK TO THE SURFACE...TO THE CLIENT...
I WAS TOLD THAT AN ADVENTURER IN FULL PLATE ARMOR WOULD HAVE THE PACKAGE AT A BAR DOWN HERE.
ALL I HAD TO DO FROM THERE WAS SAY THE PASSWORD AND TAKE IT.
EMPLOYING TWO ADVEN-TURERS FOR DIFFERENT ROLES, FROM DIFFERENT FAMILIAS EVEN...
WHO... WAS THE CLIENT?
...I DON'T KNOW.

R-REALLY, I DON'T!
IT HAPPENED A LITTLE WHILE AGO ON A DESERTED STREET IN THE MIDDLE OF THE NIGHT.
SOMEONE IN A PITCH-BLACK ROBE, MAN OR WOMAN, I'M NOT SURE, SHOWED UP OUT OF NOWHERE.
OF COURSE I WAS SUSPICIOUS, BUT...THE REWARD...AND THE UPFRONT MONEY WERE TOO GOOD TO PASS UP.
PATA (WAG)
PATA
WHAT?
BUT LULUNE-SAN, YOU'RE LEVEL TWO, AREN'T YOU?
WOULDN'T IT BE DANGEROUS FOR YOU TO TRAVEL TO THE TOWN OF RIVIRA ALONE?
!
GIKU (TWITCH)
Y...YOU SEE, UM... HERMES-SAMA TOLD ME TO HIDE MY LEVEL...
ACTU-ALLY... I'M LEVEL THREE.
......
......
AIZ-SAN, WE SHOULD REALLY LET THE CAPTAIN KNOW...
NO!!
THERE ARE TOO MANY PEOPLE!
I'M SURE HASHANA'S KILLER IS STILL AROUND!
AND IF THEY FIND OUT I HAVE THE PACKAGE, THIS TIME I'LL BE THE ONE WHO...!?

……
……
GIVE US THE PACKAGE.
...
GATA (SHAKE)
GATA
!!
GOSO (GRAB)
I WAS TOLD NOT TO ASK QUESTIONS AND TO NEVER SHOW ANYONE ELSE, BUT...
……!
WH-WHAT IS THAT ...!?

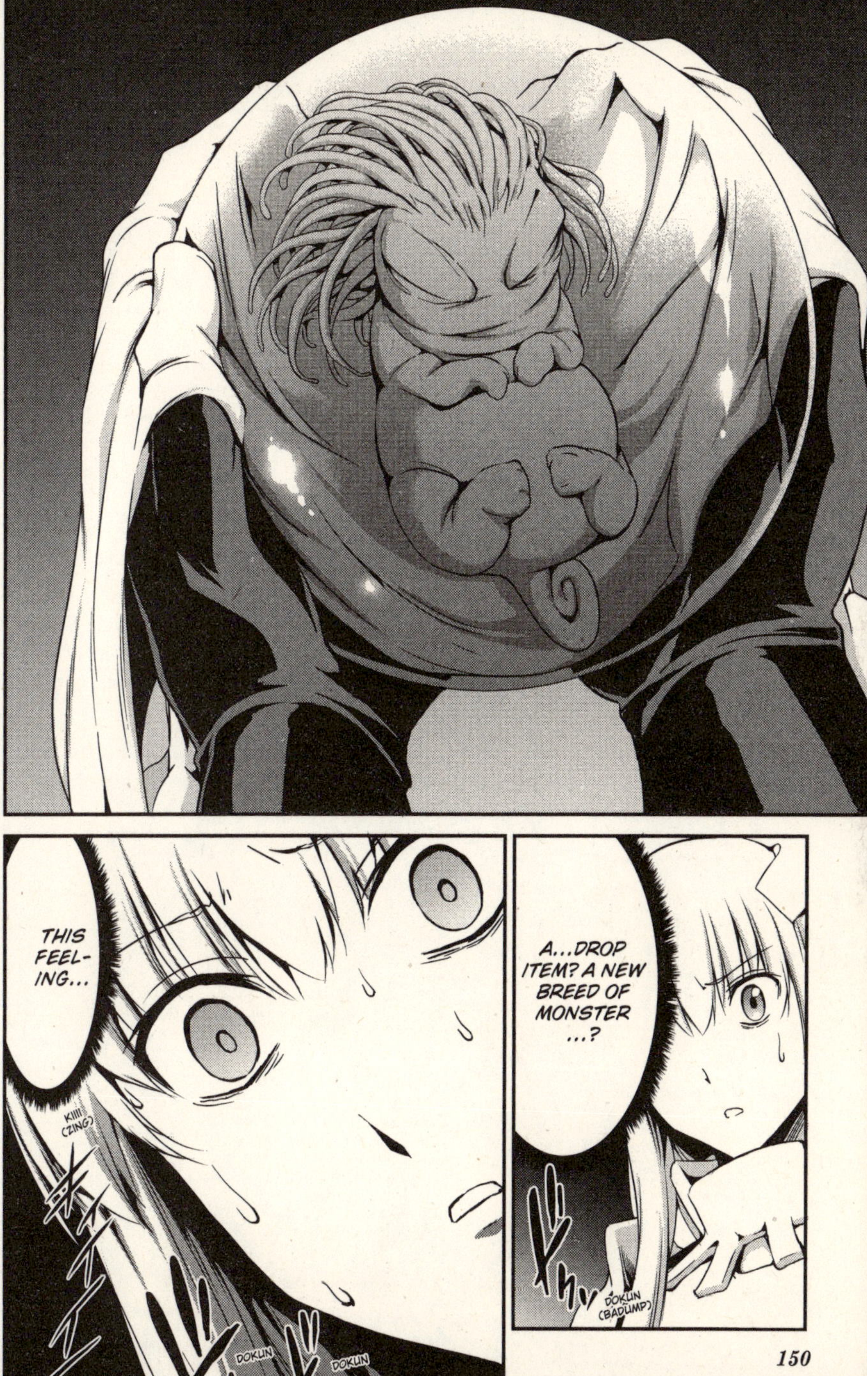
A...DROP ITEM? A NEW BREED OF MONSTER ...?
DOKUN (BADUMP)
THIS FEEL-ING...
KIIII (ZING)
DOKUN
DOKUN

FU
(WOBBLE)
AIZ-
SAN
!?
WHAT IS
THIS...?

... THERE YOU ARE.
—COME.
GOBO (BLUB)
PYUIIIII (HOWL)

ARE YOU ALL RIGHT, AIZ-SAN...?
...YES. FINE.
F-FINE? YOU SURE DON'T LOOK LIKE IT...
I SHOULD'VE KNOWN THIS THING WAS BAD NEWS!!
IT... SEEMS TO HAVE NO ADVERSE EFFECT ON ME WHEN I HOLD IT...
...DOES IT HAVE AN ADVERSE EFFECT ON HUMANS? OR PER-HAPS...
SU (SHF)
WHATEVER THE CASE, SOMETHING TELLS ME TO NOT LET AIZ-SAN NEAR IT...!
I WILL DELIVER THIS TO THE CAPTAIN!!
SORRY, LEFIYA...
PLEASE DO NOT APOLOGIZE. I WILL DO WHAT I MUST AT TIMES LIKE THIS...
WELL THEN, LET'S GO—
DOOON (KABOOM)

AREN'T THOSE ...!?

オオオオオオ
OOOOO
(ROAR)

WHO THE HELL LET MONSTERS IN HERE!?
WHAT ARE THE LOOKOUTS DOING!!?
WAAAH!
WAAAH!
TIONA, TIONE, PROTECT THEM!!
ON IT!!
YOU GOT IT!!
BO (F-WOOSH)
BO
FIRST MONSTER-PHILIA, AND NOW HERE? WHERE DO THESE THINGS COME FROM!?
EVERY-ONE, STAY WITH THE GROUP!!

RIVERIA, THE CREATURES RESPOND TO MAGIC ENERGY.
TRY TO DRAW AS MANY AS YOU CAN THIS WAY WITH YOUR MAGIC!
UNDER-STOOD.
BORS, GET EVERYONE INTO FIVE-MEMBER BATTLE PARTIES!
HAVE EACH PARTY ENGAGE ONE OF THE CREATURES!
Y-YEAH!
!!
!!
DA (DASH)

GYA
(LUNGE)
GA
(SLAM)
RU
(WHIRL)
THIS IS TOO PERFECT...
NO MONSTERS ARE BORN ON THIS FLOOR—IT'S A SAFE POINT.
WHICH MEANS THESE PLANT MONSTERS CAME UP FROM A DIFFERENT FLOOR, SURROUNDED THE TOWN, AND STAYED HIDDEN.
GUIIN
(BEND)

IT'S TOO COORDINATED TO BE A COINCIDENCE!
BA (LAUNCH)
BI (SHING)
PACHI (WINK)
!

TA (DASH)
SIGN: FESTIVAL
MONSTER-PHILIA.
AN EVENT WHERE ADVENTURERS TAME MONSTERS IN FRONT OF A LIVE AUDIENCE.
THE MONSTERS THAT ATTACKED AIZ... ...SOMEBODY WAS PULLIN' THE STRINGS.
WHICH LEADS ME TO BELIEVE SOMETHING IS ABOUT TO HAPPEN.
TA
TA
TA
TA
ZA (SLIDE)

IS IT EVEN POSSIBLE ...!?
CONTROLLING THIS MANY MONSTERS AT ONCE!?
IT'S HARD TO BELIEVE.
BUT THERE'S NO OTHER EXPLANATION.
THE MURDERER MUST BE A TAMER...!!

ZAN (SLASH)
BI (SLICE)
DOOON (BOOM)
THANK YOU, AIZ-SAN!
Y-YOU'VE GOTTA BE KID-DING!?
THEY'RE COMING FROM OVER THERE TOO!!
OOOOO (HOWL)
LEFIYA, GET TO THE SQUARE!
AIZ-SAN!?
ZUDAN (THUD)

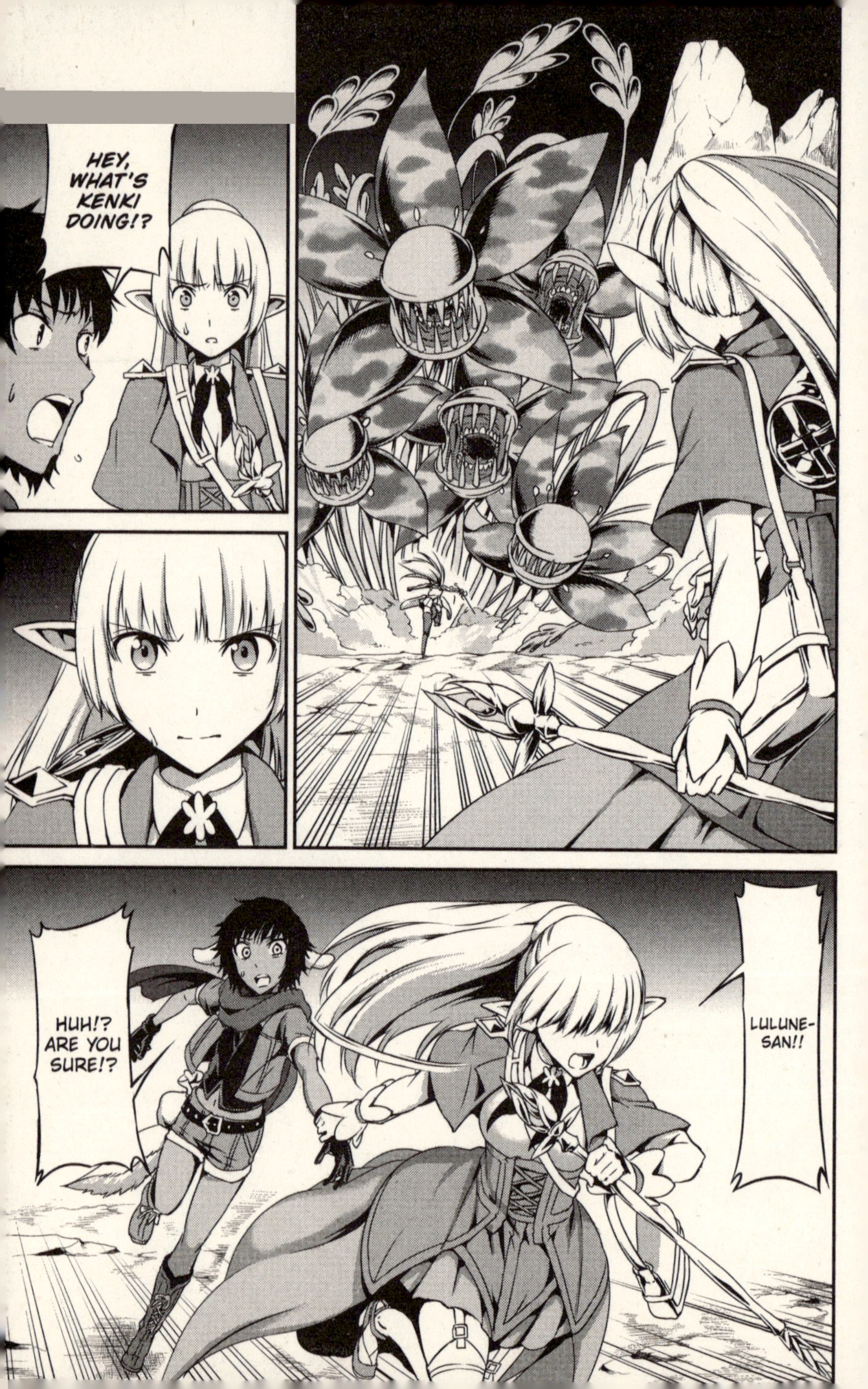
HEY, WHAT'S KENKI DOING!?
LULUNE-SAN!!
HUH!? ARE YOU SURE!?

THOSE ENEMY MONSTERS MOST LIKELY EXCEED LEVEL THREE.
LULUNE-SAN AND I ALONE WOULDN'T BE ABLE TO PROTECT OURSELVES.
AT THE SAME TIME, MORE PLANT MONSTERS WILL CONVERGE ON MY MAGIC ENERGY SHOULD I BEGIN CASTING.
MY PRESENCE HERE WILL ONLY HOLD AIZ-SAN BACK!
WHAT I MUST DO FOR HER RIGHT NOW IS...
...DELIVER THE ORB AND LULUNE-SAN TO THE OTHERS!!
THAT IS ALL I CAN POSSIBLY DO NOW!!

GO
(BANG)
W-WAS THAT... A-AN EXPLOSION!?
THAT WAS... RIVERIA-SAMA'S MAGIC!
GASHA
(STOMP)
...!?

GASHAN (CLANK)
GASHAN
GASHAN
GASHAN
A MALE ADVENTURER...?
THEN AGAIN ...

S-STOP RIGHT THERE!!
BA (THRUST)
GA
SHA (CREAK)
DON (WHAM)
!!!

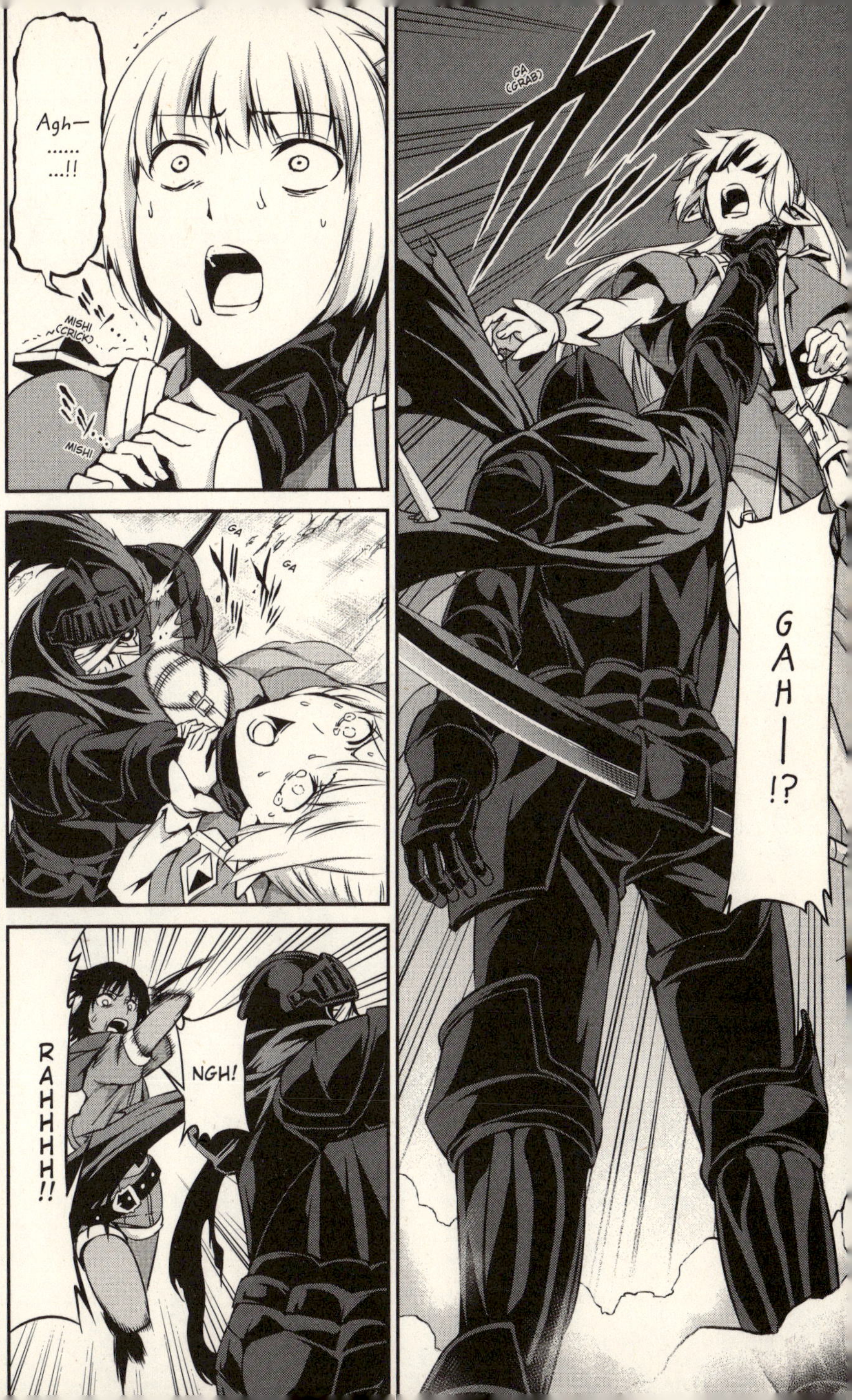
GA (GRAB)
GAH—!?
Agh— ....!!
MISHI (CRICK)
MISHI
GA
GA
RAHHHHH!!
NGH!

GO
(SLAM)
GAAH!
ZUZU
(SLIP)
—AIZ...
SAN.
MEKII
(CRACK)

GOGA (CRASH)
BO (WHOOSH)

DONN (THUD)
GA (SHING)
KAN (CLATTER)
KA
ZA (SLIDE)
LEFIYA, ARE YOU OKAY?
COUGH! COUGH!
Y... YES!

...ARE YOU THE ONE WHO KILLED HASHANA-SAN?
!!
WHAT IF I AM?
THAT'S A WOM-AN'S VOICE!!
YOU'RE NOT A MAN...!?
ZAAA (WHOOSH)
I JUST PEELED IT OFF.

I JUST PEELED OFF THE FACE OF A CORPSE. NOW I'M WEARING IT.
MICHI (TUG)
INJECTING A DEAD BODY WITH "POISON VERMIS" PREVENTS SKIN DECAY.
... DIDN'T YOU KNOW?
SO, THAT WAS HASHANA-SAN'S...?
AH, SCREW THIS!
GASHAN (CLANG)
GASHA (CLATTER)
TOO FRICKIN' TIGHT.
KA (CLACK)

NOW THEN.
I WILL BE TAKING THE SEED.
ZURUU (DRAG)
SHE'S GONE—!?
FU (WHOOSH)
DA (BAM)

GO (BOOM)
SO YOU ARE STRONG!
ZERI (SHAKE)
ZERI
!!

GIKI (RATTLE)
PARRIED!!
KUN (WHOOSH)
BI (SLASH)

BO
(WHAM)

GA (CLANG)
GA
GA
GA
GA
GA
GA
GYA (PULL)
BUN (SWOOSH)
GO (SLAM)

DOKYU (BOOM)
GAGAGAGA (SCREECH)
SHE'S STRONG !!
HOW COULD I NOT KNOW THIS ADVENTURER'S NAME? SOMEONE WITH THIS MUCH PROWESS!?
BIRI BIRI (TINGLE)

Unleashed pillar of light, limbs of the holy tree. You are the master archer.
BA (DASH)
Loose your arrows, fairy archers.
Pierce, arrows of accu-racy!!

DOU
(BOOM)
ARCS RAY!!
A SINGLE TARGET SPELL WHERE THE GOAL IS SPEED.
HOWEVER, IT'S SPECIAL IN THAT IT PURSUES THE TARGET.
ONCE FIRED, THE ENEMY CANNOT EVADE!!
IT WILL NEVER MISS!!!

DON (BANG)
HOW COULD ANYONE TAKE THAT AND—!!?
JIJII (SIZZLE)

BOKYU (WHOOSH)
DON
KIKIKI (RUMBLE)
EEEEK!!

LEFI—
...
URK—!!
BUKI
(SLASH)

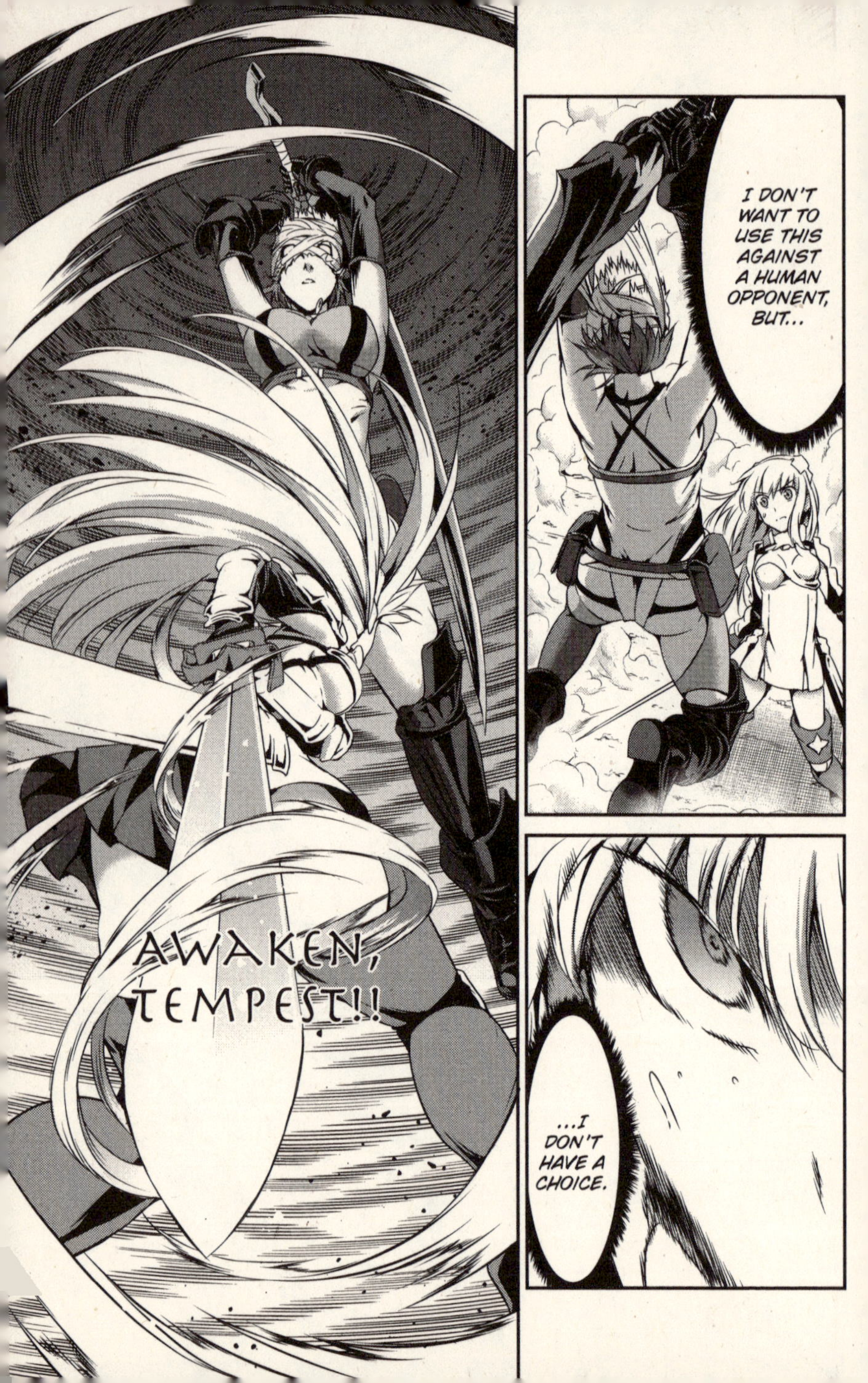
I DON'T WANT TO USE THIS AGAINST A HUMAN OPPONENT, BUT...
...I DON'T HAVE A CHOICE.
AWAKEN, TEMPEST!!

GOU
(RUMBLE)

GA
GA
GA
GA
GA
GA (SLIDE)
HAA!
HAA!
HAA!
......
......
AHH ...
...NEVER THOUGHT I'D FIND TWO THINGS I'M AFTER AT THE SAME TIME.
GARA (SLIP)
THAT WIND ...
SO THEN ...
BORO (FLOP)
PARA (FWP)
PARA

...YOU MUST BE "ARIA."

KATA (TREMBLE)
KATA
KATA
?
AIZ-SAN...?
HAA.
HAA.
KATA
KATA
HOW...HOW DO YOU KNOW...?
THE ONLY ONES WHO KNOW ABOUT THAT ARE...
THERE COULDN'T BE ANYONE ELSE...!
WHO... ARE YOU?

WHO ARE YOU!!?
Sword Oratoria 3 End

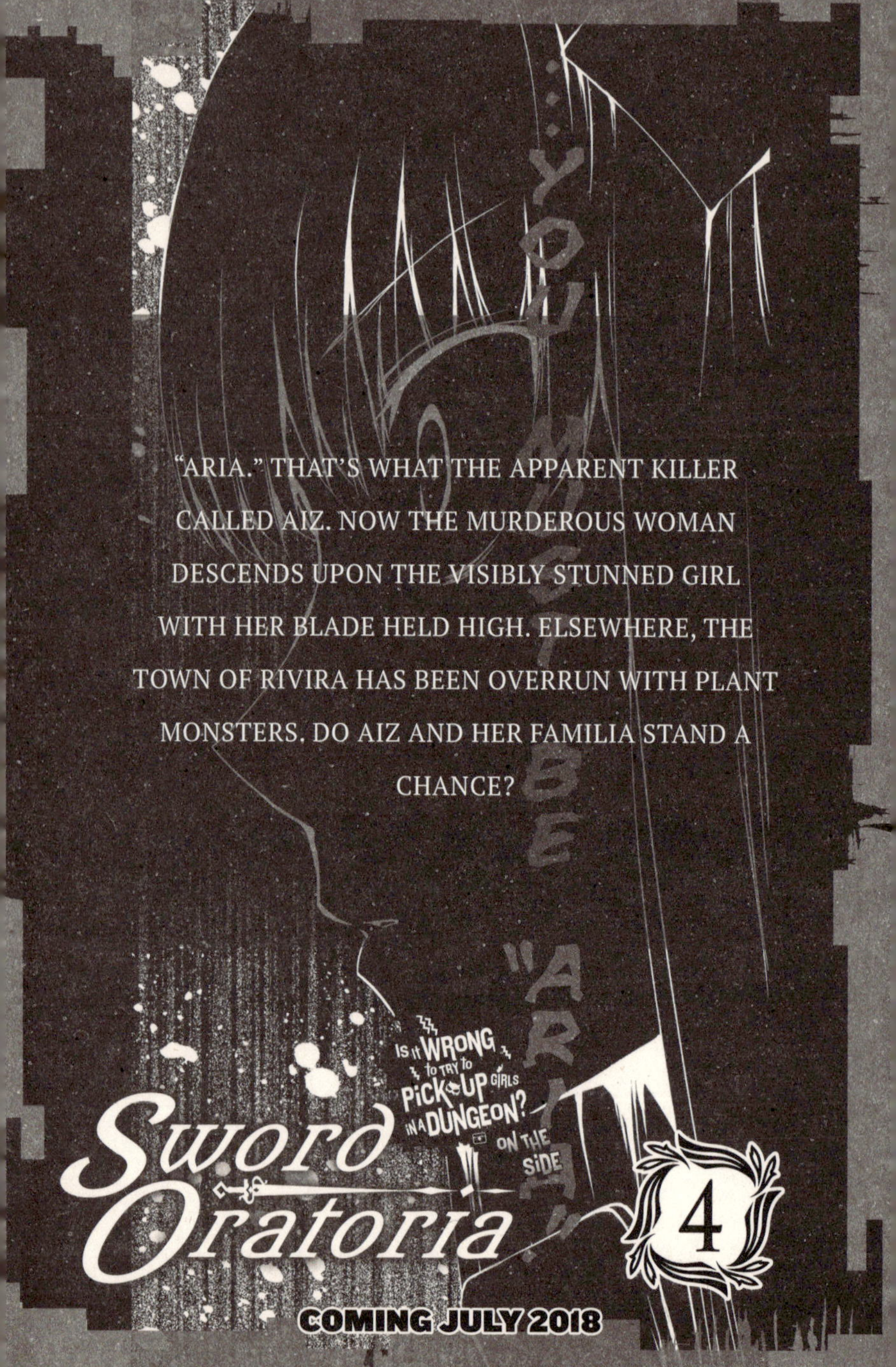
"ARIA." THAT'S WHAT THE APPARENT KILLER CALLED AIZ. NOW THE MURDEROUS WOMAN DESCENDS UPON THE VISIBLY STUNNED GIRL WITH HER BLADE HELD HIGH. ELSEWHERE, THE TOWN OF RIVIRA HAS BEEN OVERRUN WITH PLANT MONSTERS. DO AIZ AND HER FAMILIA STAND A CHANCE?
YOU MUST BE "ARIA"!
IS IT WRONG TO TRY TO PICK UP GIRLS IN A DUNGEON? ON THE SIDE
Sword Oratoria
4
COMING JULY 2018

THIS IS TODAY'S BONUS COMIC.

ATTACKERS
AIZ, TIONA, TIONE, BETE
ABLE TO MOVE INDEPENDENTLY UNDER FINN'S DIRECT ORDERS. DUTIES INCLUDE PRIORITIZING PARTICULARLY DANGEROUS MONSTERS AND KEEPING LARGE GROUPS IN CHECK TO ALLOW THE FRONT LINE A CHANCE TO REGROUP.
EACH MEMBER MUST POSSESS THE STRENGTH TO ONE-SHOT MONSTERS, THE SPEED TO CROSS THE BATTLEFIELD IN THE BLINK OF AN EYE, AND THE ENDURANCE TO KEEP RUNNING AT FULL SPEED THROUGHOUT THE BATTLE. ONLY LEVEL-FIVE ADVENTURERS CAN FILL THIS ROLE.
SINCE HEAVY ARMOR WOULD WEIGH THEM DOWN AND RESTRICT THEIR MOVEMENTS, PROTECTIVE EQUIPMENT IS KEPT TO A MINIMUM.
ARTILLERY
LEFIYA, 1-3 OTHERS
POSITIONED ON THE LEFT AND RIGHT FLANKS OF THE FRONT LINE, THEY ARE TASKED WITH ELIMINATING MONSTERS THAT TRY TO CIRCUMVENT THE FORMATION.
ビーム BIMU (BEAM)
LEFIYA MAINLY RELIES ON HER SHORT TRIGGER SPELL "ARCS RAY" TO ELIMINATE MONSTERS AND CONTROL THE FLOW OF BATTLE.
RESERVES
RAUL AND SEVERAL OTHERS
THEY PROVIDE SUPPORT WHEREVER FINN DEEMS IT NECESSARY.
UNLIKE THE ATTACKERS, THEY MOVE TO HEAL WOUNDED ALLIES WHILE ASSISTING IN OTHER PARTS OF THE BATTLEFIELD AS A UNIT.
THEY PROVIDE RANGED SUPPORT FROM THE BACK LINE UNTIL ORDERED ELSEWHERE.
COMMANDER
FINN
AT THE CENTER OF THE FORMATION, IT'S HIS RESPONSIBILITY NOT ONLY TO ISSUE ORDERS WITH HIS VOICE BUT TO SIGNAL HIS ALLIES WITH THE FAMILIA'S FLAG.
(WHOOSH)
REAR
RIVERIA, OTHER MAGIC USERS
PROTECT THE FRONT LINE WITH MAGIC SPELLS FROM A DISTANCE.
RIVERIA FOCUSES SOLELY ON CASTING A SPELL THAT WILL END THE BATTLE.
FRONT LINE
GARETH AND 10-20 OTHERS
WITH LEVEL-SIX GARETH AT THE POINT POSITION, THEY BECOME RIVERIA'S SHIELD UNTIL HER WIDE-RANGE SPELL IS READY.
THEY PRIORITIZE FORMING A WALL OVER SLAYING MONSTERS, SO EACH IS EQUIPPED WITH HEAVY ARMOR AND A THICK SHIELD.
SO YOU SEE, I DREW THIS SCENE KEEPING IN MIND THAT LOKI FAMILIA MAXIMIZES THEIR LEVEL-FIVE ADVENTURERS' BATTLE CAPABILITIES WHILE KEEPING ORARIO'S STRONGEST MAGIC USER AS SAFE AS POSSIBLE DURING COMBAT.
...DID YA NOW?
SURE SOUNDS LIKE YA MADE IT UP AFTER THE FACT TO ME.
...!!
GIKURI (SHUDDER)
ニヤ... NYA (GRIN)
SEE YOU IN VOLUME 4!!
BYE!
TO BE CONTINUED